Fantsy

Amelia Surprised

Novella. Choosing to have a subsequent kid was the simple part.

Louise Burton

* Chapter 1 *

"She will take an interest in the Solstice festivity? Huh!" Captain Brandon Fisher turned his seat and gazed out from his second-story window, watching the occasion swarms clamor along Snapdragon Street. Some went east to the close-by business sectors. However, most traveled west to the celebrations. "When did you discover?"

"A tiny bit of spot prior." Jaime Starshine, Lieutenant of the Household Guard, watched her commander thoughtfully. His voice was quiet. However, Jaime wasn't tricked. Earthy colored hair, earthy colored eyes, clean-cut, and mediocre tallness, he effectively passed as normal, even forgettable; however, that mixing out of the spotlight was intentional. Frequently the best gatekeeper is the one you didn't see. When he provided orders, individuals complied, and when there was an inconvenience, there was no mixing up his position. Brandon had an order presence. However, when the circumstance called for covertness, she had seen him be unpretentious, or when essential, quick and deadly. She realized he was more seasoned than the thirty years he looked, yet she didn't know exactly the number of had been eradicated by enchantment. Jaime proceeded with her report. "From the start, Her Ladyship needed to go alone. However, I persuaded her it was certifiably not a smart thought. Now and again, the outsiders don't take 'no' for an answer. Nora Carpenter is going with her."

Brandon bounced up, turning on her. "Nora! She's in the civilian army, with just a year of excellent preparation. It's Summer Solstice in the capital and the greatest occasion of the year! All the vermin in the city will be out!"

"If she weren't qualified, you wouldn't have recruited her. She may lose her wallet. However, she will secure the wrongdoing Duchess, the beneficiary obvious, with her life." Jaime was undaunted by either his glare or his upheaval. "I think Her Ladyship speculates you threatened the last couple of men she was keen on."

"I didn't."

"You did as such! I was there when you conveyed her blessing to the last one, recall? Pleasant, you were. At that point, you broke the sculpture in his hall with a solitary strike of your hand. 'I would take a dreary perspective on any individual who hurt this lady.' The man pissed his jeans!"

"So he did." A grin pulled at the sides of his mouth, destroying his hot air. "You're certain she will wear the dress?"

"I saw her draw it from the capacity chest myself."

Brandon moved back to his work area and set aside the log books, glaring. "I can't secure her if she will not disclose to me where she's going. Much thanks to you, Lieutenant. That will be all."

He looked into when she didn't leave, his eyebrows raised.

"Skipper . . . Brandon, why not reveal to her how you feel?"

"What are you discussing?"

"For as long as a year, both of you have been battling a great deal. Furthermore, not simply the sort of quarrels that occasionally occur between companions. In any event, it isn't so much that way any longer. It's getting tedious sneaking around here. I'm by all accounts not the only one who's seen. I've presented with you for a very long time at this point, and we've endured some very difficult spots. That excursion to the mausoleums makes me cold to my bones, and you got over it like it was nothing. However, with regards to revealing to her your sentiments, you delay. Why? You love her. Disclose to her how you feel!"

"It isn't so straightforward."

"Why not? Since she's Duke Thorband's little girl? Since she's a mage? Titles are accursed. Under, she's a lady, and you are a man. She has the right to know how you feel."

Brandon gazed at her. "OK," he said finally. "I'll converse with her. Disclose to Nora our conversation may take some time, so if Lady Amelia doesn't appear acceptable away, not to come searching for her, but rather to be accessible when she calls."

* Chapter 2 *

Sharaton-Charlottesville. Twin clamoring urban areas isolated by Lucky Man River, a toward the north streaming slow stream traversed various occasions by wide extensions before joining a lot bigger Crescent River similarly as it turned east toward the sea. The urban areas were established in 2020 by Prince Caernach Moramorian and his two spouses, Shara and Charlotte. The little estate was changed when the two ladies were announced holy people by their goddess and Lawgiver, Rena. Once, far toward the north, a long ways past the Skyreach Mountains, lived a great many roaming Ba'lorians – individuals of dalendan Bannan Lorrie or the sacrosanct Earth Mother. They assembled at the summons of their Lawgiver, and in an incredible movement enduring a year, traveled south. These equivalent thousands showed up not long after the principal house being finished was taken as a feature of their goddess's astuteness. The heads of the Great Houses swore their allegiance to House Moramorian, set apart our pastures for their groups, plowed new ranches, and filled the new urban communities of Sharaton and Charlottesville craftsmen and laborers.

Inside twenty years, different urban areas were as excitedly slashed from the wild. Ramez and Crystal Tide toward the upper east inside the Duchy of Atansha, Rondar, and Barter Town in the Duchy of Beyjure Keen toward the middle. Winged serpent Keep in the Principality of Brotava toward the northwest. Goodfellow Keep and City of the Suns in the Duchy of Biyandi. Southeast, on the mouth of the Crescent, discharging into the Great Eastern Ocean, was Portsmouth in the Duchy of Zashandi. Tilda turned into an overwhelming youthful realm cut out of the wild, and Sharaton-Charlottesville its clamoring capital.

The Ba'lorians constructed immense sanctuary compounds in Charlottesville, smaller than normal urban communities in themselves, committed to the four individuals from the blessed family. Rena, wind goddess and Lawgiver, whom they worshiped most, was given a straightforward outside stone-shrouded structure. Her dad, Auros, expert of the time, had a little sanctuary neighboring. To Li Var Dayanna, the earth goddess and Rena's mom, and Rena's more youthful sibling, Osh Mayan, divine force of waters, ripeness, and mending, they devoted gigantic rambling constructions. The Laws deserved admiration for the Earth Mother, and Her kin complied. The Temple of Osh Mayan managed the Rites of Adulthood, offered sexual types of assistance for an ostensible charge, and were known as committed healers of psyche, body, and soul.

As the years passed, the country of Tildor flourished. Pulled in by the riches and imperativeness, Hellenic and Kemetic outsiders from the far off, western Caloren States, and Celts from the southern wilderlands streamed in for their offer. A peace agreement was reached with Woodhaven, their closest neighbor and home of the mythical foresty people.

For a long time, trains employed the Royal Roads, bringing the realm ever more major development and thriving. Crowds and homesteads thrived, and after the subsequent decade, artworks and expressions and afterward valuable metals were to be found in bounty. In the second year of the twenty-second century, the capital's consolidated populace added up to almost a hundred thousand, the greater part of whom were human.

Consistently, Osh Mayan's sanctuaries offered recuperating and sexual types of assistance as a trade-off for gifts. 'Sanctuary conceived' youngsters are coming about because these associations were authentic, both by custom and law, every kid adding to the House Rolls of their mom's group.

The summer solstice was the greatest occasion, with ten days of celebrations committed to the occasion. The outsiders in the city all had their solstice festivities – the Kemetics with the Bull of Abydos and celebration of Osiris, the Hellenes with Demeter, and the Bacchanale Celts with their huge fires, their singing, and moving. The Ba'lorians regarded their earth goddess for Her job as a supplier and as the exemplification of parenthood. It was additionally an opportunity to give recognition to the male standard as the wellspring of maternity. During the summer solstice, a lady keen on childbearing didn't need to go to Son's sanctuary. Or maybe, by custom, she wore a bright blue dress and a wide red band to show her sexual accessibility. Those not inspired by such exercises abstained from wearing blue dresses during the celebration or gambled being greeted by guys pulled in by the clothing.

Men who delighted in these contacts were honest to make a gift subsequently to the sanctuary. Most did, for it was viewed as misfortune to slight the divine beings. The lady consistently reserved the privilege to reject coupling with anybody or under any conditions she didn't care for.

No implied no. The law was severe on that. Assault under Ba'lorian law, except if the casualty picked something else, conveyed capital punishment. It was uncommon for the clanswoman, who implemented the law, to make do with less.

Ten years sooner, with an end goal to lessen the rate of assault, particularly from outsiders who didn't comprehend the solstice customs or the law, Queen Dorothy had restricted the sexual celebrations to a ten square territory in the midtown area. To build up the all-around furnished constabulary, both the military and local army enhanced the regular watches. It was reinforced by youthful ministers and hero priests from the Ba'lorian sanctuaries. This change brought about fewer attacks, and soon comparative limitations were set up all through the realm.

When she was eighteen, Amelia Starshine, a third girl of Duke Thorband Starshine, went through her Rite of Adulthood. For about fourteen days, she took in the assortments and intricacies of sex, pleasuring, and how to direct pregnancy at the sanctuary of Osh Mayan alongside the other youthful Ba'lorians of her age gathering. Endurance was the second piece of the Ritual. In the same way as other different sets, Amelia and her accomplice, Dalyan Dawnslight, outfitted and provided distinctly with what they could convey, went into the wild for the following thirty days. Amelia endure. Dalyan Dawnslight, her sweetheart, didn't.

Soon after her return and before her grieving was finished, Amelia requested to turn into her mom's hidden disciple. Duchess Dianne Starshine, a high priestess of Rena just as an expert in the Northern Star Order of Magic, was astonished by the solicitation. Regardless she acknowledged her girl as a student.

The accompanying six years of Amelia's life were seriously overwhelmed by the extended periods important to learning magic, for the duchess was both unstinting and requesting in her job as an instructor. Not long before her investigations were finished, nonetheless, and against the urging of her folks, Amelia put on the blue dress and red band and burned through every one of the tens of the Solstice occasions in the wild festival. Amelia's girl, named Dalyanni after her lost darling, was brought into the world nine months after the fact. As Amelia, the youngster was smooth-cleaned, tanned, blonde, with huge green eyes.

When her examinations were finished, Amelia attempted some difficult missions for her dad, Duke Thorband, leader of Biyandi. These undertakings expanded her ability and comprehension of enchantment, with the additional advantage of enormously extending her very own abundance.

However, within four years, she started to feel fretful, wanting to turn out to be more free. Amelia got together her girl and developing individual family and set off for the capital and the imperial court, governed by her mom's more seasoned sister, Queen Dorothy. Her folks energized her, demanding that she compose frequently and make regular return visits with their granddaughter.

On her mom's suggestion, Amelia and her family went with a youthful half-mythical person as of late wedded to three sisters, Tia, Tahna, and Mindal Landers. The attractive half-mythical person, Reison Whisper Wind, was appallingly youthful and unpracticed, yet he was given to his new ladies. Mindal, the most youthful, a versifier of incredible ability and rather celebrated, engaged them as they voyaged. Tia, the most established, was a high priestess to Rena and of chapel rank almost equivalent to Duchess Dianne herself. Tahna, the leftover sister, was a fighter priest of extraordinary expertise, known for dealing with crooks. Tia and Tahna were less notable to the overall population. However, both included notorieties inside the congregation for fixing troublesome issues.

Little Dalyanni was charmed with the excursion to the capital, however considerably more so with Reison. At camp every evening, she floated around the youthful half-mythical being, handling him with inquiries until her eyes could presently don't remain open. Amelia attempted to debilitate Dalyanni's connection. However, Reison approached her girl's considerations with deference and graciousness.

Partially through their excursion, the four-year-old young lady intensely requested that Reison add Amelia as his fourth spouse so he could turn into her dad. Amelia almost passed on from shame. Reison amenably yet solidly declined. The three sisters, as far as it matters for them, responded with incredible delight. However, it was a reminder for Amelia. She understood how much a void her enchanted investigations and adventuring had left in her daughter's life. From that point on, she made plans to go through, in any event, an hour every day of individual time with her youngster.

A kinship bloomed between the explorers, and to their common enjoyment, the Whisper Wind love birds found a spot inside a kilometer of Amelia's new house in Sharaton-Charlottesville. Both were inside a brief distance of the Sandhurst College of Music, the possible objective of Reison Whisper Wind.

As Dalyanni developed more established, the day by day time Amelia went through with her effectively fortified the connection between them. Despite this, nonetheless, Dalyanni's desire for a dad just expanded as the years passed. Inside the previous year, Reison educated Amelia that her ten-year-old girl was halting by after school to visit him – still focused on his parental prospects.

Amelia's intensifying issue, following six years of marriage, the three sisters had a few upbeat kids, and Reison transparently cherished his spouses and his kids. At the point when Reison received the girl of their tutor, Dalyanni was euphoric. On their next visit to the

Whisper Wind family a few days after the fact, Dalyanni moved toward Reison for a similar advantage. He liberally concurred, however, just if Amelia was willing.

For Amelia, as enticing as it may have been to give her little girl the dad figure she so clearly required, the possibility was overwhelming. Regardless of whether Reison's full house might have included her own family, she had no interest in being engaged with a confounded conjugal plan.

Various marriage game plans could work and even be glad more often than not, and the Whisper Wind family itself was simply such a model. It helped, however, that the three sisters had not just experienced childhood in such a family themselves, yet that they were likewise genuinely dedicated to one another. Not every person changed well to sharing mates, nonetheless, and the more accomplices in the relationship, the more delicate it was.

Confounding the issue further, Tia Whisper Wind had become Amelia's compatriot and minister questioner.

Tahna, while not, at this point a champion priest, had since become an associate with whom she sought after esoteric exploration. Despite her kinships with the three sisters – she loved them hugely – Amelia wasn't keen on turning into Reison's fourth spouse. While she questioned they would treat her inadequately, it would put her most minimal in position. More, she enjoyed Reison all around ok yet was not pulled into him. What's more, none of that even though that Amelia would one day acquire the Duchy of Biyandi and City of the Suns, its flourishing capital.

She was additionally reluctant to acknowledge the other option, for the reception would mean Dalyanni is leaving her home and moving in with the Whisper Wind family. Amelia considered the possibility of her little girl leaving intolerable and denied the solicitation.

Dalyanni sobbed for quite a long time.

While Amelia worried over what to do, Captain Brandon Fisher ventured into the pained young lady's life, investing hours at energy with Dalyanni, even expressly accompanying her to and from school. Amelia was alleviated, for it additionally finished Dalyanni's unapproved after-school hikes. Before long, the empty eyes vanished, and her steady prattling returned.

A little while later, curious, Amelia proposed the matter with her girl.

"I'm fine, Mother," Dalyanni replied. "I didn't care for it. However, you are the parent. I comprehend that at this point." Her self-evident truth answer satisfied Amelia extraordinarily. "Other than," her ten-year-old girl proceeded, "I sorted out how Reison Whisper Wind can, in any case, turn into my Dad. At the point when I grow up, I'll wed his child, Steve."

"Dalyanni," Amelia figured out how to gag out, "that is not a valid justification to get hitched. Additionally, it's not reasonable for Steve."

"Why not?"

"Indeed, there are numerous motivations to get hitched; however, the best one is for affection. Be that as it may, on the off chance that you can't wed for adoration, at any rate, wed somebody who will regard you and your youngsters and who will be a decent supplier."

"In any case, I do like Steve. What's more, Mr. Murmur Wind will show Steve how to be a decent Dad."

Intrigued with her rationale, Amelia let the matter drop. In any case, she later gave the disclosure to Steve's folks. It was the respectable activity, she thought. When Dalyanni was more seasoned and on the off chance that she had plans for the Whisper Wind kid, he planned to require all the assist he with getting!

Occasions of the past winter, in any case, built up upon Amelia the delicacy of life and how kids were considerably more fragile than they frequently showed up. Healers, doctors, and surprisingly the clerics' tremendous force to raise the dead didn't generally keep individuals from unexpected passing, nor did it ensure life could be reestablished once lost. In any event, for the individuals who could manage the cost of the enormous costs charged by the sanctuaries – kids, particularly those more youthful than their fifth year, were famously hard to bring resurrected.

The latest winter had seen a progression of hard tempests cover Sharaton-Charlottesville under a few feet of snow. Inside seven days of the storm, a flare-up of Aurora Madness moved through a few areas, including their own. It was profoundly infectious and enchanted in nature; it wracked the casualty with serious bone agony for up to a month while rainbow tones sparkled across their skin. Ministers of adequate experience could fix the infection; however, treatment was restricted to keeping them hydrated and took care of for most. All things being equal, it killed many, and in some cases, the individuals who endure were broken as a main priority, getting either completely aloof or crazy and risky. An isolated spell from the Queen's Lord High Wizard invalidated all movement sorcery inside the city to hold the infection back from spreading to different urban communities in the realm or different countries. All types of mysterious entryways, gateways, and so forth essentially stopped working inside a day's movement. When Dalyanni got the Madness, Amelia couldn't transport her kid to her mom in the City of the Suns for recuperating.

Amelia got berserk sitting tight for doctors and clerics that won't ever show up between the infection and the practically ongoing surge of additional blizzards. Before the second's over the day of sickness, Dalyanni declined, the youngster's cries decreased to a consistent, dry croaking. Amelia requested the workers to wrap up her girl for the excursion to the sanctuary. Brandon smoothly advised her that Tia Whisper Wind was equipped for restoring her and that she carried on significantly closer. While Amelia followed behind, her wizardry shielding them from the tough, wounding virus winds and blinding whirlwinds, Brandon conveyed Dalyanni, clearing their way through roads that were chest-profound with snow.

Furthermore, simply that Spring, Dalyanni went to her Tenth Year preparing at the sanctuary. The graduation service was defaced by a significant seismic tremor that shook the whole city, however, the whole landmass. Thousands kicked the bucket in Sheraton-

Charlottesville, and a lot more harm, including many youngsters and their families going to the sanctuary. When her girl was protected, Amelia and her staff went through a few days assisting with saving the caught and harmed, and afterward, recuperating the dead, and with a tidy up.

When the crisis was finished and her own home fixed, Amelia took Dalyanni for a short visit to her folks. The reasoning was to move away from the still-new recollections of the mutilated bodies. Nonetheless, as they worked in her mom's broad gardens, the duchess watchfully asked Amelia what grieved her. Amelia admitted her forlornness and Dalyanni's craving for a dad. Amelia additionally needed more youngsters and a spouse to help raise them. Her endeavors, she conceded, had fizzled.

The duchess embraced her girl, brushed away tears of dissatisfaction, forlornness, and pride, and set about making a rundown of qualifying unhitched males. Amelia wasn't keen on plural marriage, so that limited the rundown a piece. Regardless of whether she didn't adore the man, he needed to have agreeable characteristics so they could, at any rate, be companions, and the man needed to regard Dalyanni. Amelia was wealthy by her own doing and beneficiary to the duchy. Wedding more than one man had the allure of both assortment and vanity. However, when her mom recommended that alternative, she challenged. She needed a relationship; she clarified, not a confounded one. Overhauling at least two spouses could turn out to be very tedious. Her girl, her obscure examinations, and running her own family promptly devoured every one of the hours of her day. It would be ideal, Amelia educated her mom, if the man of honor could coordinate into Amelia's family.

"Truly? So you need a man who will be content with you as top of the House?" The Duchess gestured with delight at the disclosure. By Ba'lorian custom, whoever was an expert of the family should be docile in the room. "Inclinations to tallness, weight, the shade of hair and eyes? What might be said about his penis? How long would it be advisable for it to be? Also, how thick?" her mom pungently asked.

"Thickness is pleasant," Amelia conceded, becoming blood red. "Be that as it may, on the off chance that I like the man, I don't think the other will matter such a lot."

Her mom's eyes moved joyfully. "I'm happy to see you are reasonable. However, it may have been fun disclosing why I needed to inspect such countless youngsters and their individuals to your dad. 'Thorband, my adoration, this is for our girl,' I'd say. 'She merits legitimate fulfillment from her mate. Normally, I'll need to confirm any cases myself.'"

Amelia snickered at the fanciful scene, and that's just the beginning, so since, in such a case that Amelia had mentioned it, her mom may have done it! Sometime before she'd wedded Duke Thorband Starshine, the duchess had labored for quite a long while as a sex educator at the capital, in the sanctuary of Osh Mayan.

The duchess embraced her little girl energetically, kissing her brow. "Okay, my dear. I'll tell you when I've tracked down some forthcoming admirers."

Weeks passed, with a few lunch meetings and supper gatherings persevered through, all with no worthy possibilities. Amelia gradually developed more disillusioned and baffled, and before the month's over, she got together her little girl and transported home.

Only two days before the mid-year solstice festivities, Amelia visited the Whisper Wind family. She discovered that the Whisper Wind tutor, Dalinda Brightburr, anticipated wearing the blue dress and red band with the point of making a subsequent youngster. An endeavored raid half a month sooner by the tutor had brought about progresses from a not exactly good wizard and only days sooner, finished in a savage mystical fight inside the Whisper Wind home over Dalinda's opportunity. While the wounds and broad harm to the family had been handily fixed with enchantment, the family was worried about Dalinda's security. The wizard, Amelia was guaranteed, had been appropriately rebuffed for his deeds, yet Tia at that point referenced her concern for Dalinda's impending outing. Without really thinking, Amelia elected to go with the tutor to the grown-up just territory. Charmed, Tia convinced Dalinda to acknowledge Amelia's proposal of escort. Amelia vowed to show up before the expected time on the principal morning of the solstice occasions.

Drive, Amelia acknowledged, was a chance. Game plans were made, and Amelia took Dalyanni to visit her grandparents until the festivals were finished. Two family monitors came to help keep Dalyanni out of underhandedness.

When home, Amelia tunneled through dusty chests until she tracked down her dress and band. Her choice to accompany Dalinda had roused Amelia. Following quite a while of dozing alone, she craved the vibe of a man's hug, having one's breasts manipulated and areolas sucked, pussy licked, and the awesome, rankling delight of his hard longing blasting through her until the two of them creamed in joy. A spouse could stand by. What she needed was to get free and appropriately nailed.

Amelia attempted to put the dress on. She sadly scholarly articles of clothing that once fit enticingly couldn't be so handily worn by a thirty lady. While still as thin as she used to be, she was taller, at multiple and three-quarter meters, and she was more extensive in both her shoulders and hips. Such stature and development were not out of the ordinary. Her mom was tall, and her dad was a major man at one hundred and 98 centimeters, with the load to coordinate.

Amelia quit any pretense of attempting to pull the spruce up. Indeed, even her breasts were bigger. Some rich ladies paid wet-medical caretakers to breastfeed their youngsters. Her mom, the duchess, had demanded taking care of every one of her youngsters herself. Not long after birthing Dalyanni, another worker had asked whether Amelia wished to enlist a wet-nurture. The duchess, standing close by, said only looked so angry that the worker apologized lavishly. The subject never raised again, which was as Amelia favored it.

A minor cantrip gave the fundamental fitting changes. The roomier dress effectively passed hips and bust, settling serenely onto her shoulders. Amelia chose a light-weight, wide-overflowed cap with the warmth from the three suns outside effectively substantial through her window. Shunning a full wallet, she wrapped a little handbag cautiously inside the band. A portion of the extremely well-off went about town with no cash with the rest of their personal effects, just to demonstrate how rich they were. Amelia thought such conduct unwise and pompous.

Dressed for wanton experience, she presented in the full-length reflection. Tossing her shoulders back, her breasts rose, areolas solidifying in expectation. Amelia took a gander at herself favorably. Afterward, she thought, if the night turned out to be too cool, a shroud could be mystically brought from her stroll in the wardrobe without a lot of exertion.

Indeed, Amelia considered, this could be a truly fun day! She would get Dalinda, and they would discover a spot for breakfast before walking around a portion of the business sectors, at that point peruse the shops, allowing the tension to fabricate. After supper, they would go to the grown-ups just territory. She revealed to herself she wasn't completely dedicated at this point; however, on the off chance that she ended up tracking down a fascinating man, she was more than able to give him a lively ride, with all the vital shouting and tearing of sheets. The potential for delight conjured a jerk in her sex. The last look in her mirror demonstrated her demise.

Recollections of the solstice that made Dalyanni filled her considerations, and her soggy groin held onto control. One hand scoured her breasts and pressed her areolas while the other wound into her undies. Scouring her clit angrily, Amelia recollected the men and their hard cocks pushing profound, over and over, filling her with their seed.

Once, she had even taken on three men simultaneously. They had mounted Amelia thus, over and over, beating her sopping sex until it she was tacky with sweat and covered from tummy to ass and down to her knees with semen and her liquids. At the point when they were at last excessively spent for additional coupling, she was scarcely ready to move, considerably less walk, and her trickling pussy pulsated for quite a long time a while later.

Fingers are searching quicker; Amelia unexpectedly came, gasping and shivering. Indeed, even as her quakes blurred, the masturbation and the memory of past desire just whetted her want a more generous charge.

Removing her underwear, she utilized them to clean herself off before throwing them at the clothing hamper. Amelia fixed her dress and smiled. So imagine a scenario in which somebody sees my exposed groin. She thought.

With a feeling of developing assumption, Amelia left her suite and darted down the steps.

"Woman Amelia." Brandon Fisher appeared from an entryway, abruptly obstructing her way.

"Skipper Fisher." Less than excited, Amelia stopped, pushing out her jaw. "I'm going out, and I will be gone throughout the day, possibly more. At the point when I get back, we'll go to my folks and visit Dalyanni. Try not to hold up. I may not be back for quite a while." She moved to circumvent him.

"Indeed, Lady," he said, cutting her off the exit. "In the first place, I'd like a couple of words with you."

Amelia tightened her lips. "Indeed, Captain?"

"In your office, please. Where it will be more private."

"Great! In any case, in case you will shout at me, I will be angry with you! I have a meeting, and I don't mean to be late." Amelia turned behind her, her short dress spinning up.

Brandon saw the bare cheeks and his nose jerked at the weak fragrance. Glaring, he followed her.

Amelia inclined toward her work area as he entered her office, arms collapsed, and her foot tapping. "Indeed, Captain? What right?"

At the point when the entryway was shut, he turned, hands-on-hips. "Where do you believe you're going?"

"Assuming you're visually challenged, it's none of your damn business!" Angry, she stepped to the entryway, yet he got her wrist. "You neglect yourself!" she murmured. "Relinquish me right now!"

He shook his head. "I've failed to remember nothing. Notwithstanding, you're not going anyplace until certain things get said. I'm answerable for you and your little girl's wellbeing, Amelia. Where you go is my business! Go where you need, yet you need to disclose to me first. Is that perceived?"

Her free hand flew up, smacking him adequately across the face.

Brandon had seen it coming, her non-verbal communication and crude feeling parted with it, yet he hadn't recoiled. His cheek shading from the blow, he delivered her. "I said, is that perceived?"

"Indeed!" Amelia scoured her wrist, glaring.

"Great. Presently, where are you going?"

She feigned exacerbation. "Blue dress. Red scarf. Solstice. For what reason would you say you are in effect so thick?"

"Men will bother you, needing to couple with you." Brandon ventured close.

"They are! That is the point!"

"You need mounting? You're pretty, Amelia. Wonderful even. Long legs and brilliant hair. Numerous men will need to take you. Is that what you need? Men, to take you?" He inclined nearer, gazing eagerly at her.

"Indeed! That is the thing that I need!" She looked into, glaring resistant at him, declining to be harassed.

"Furthermore, if they put their seed inside you, you could get pregnant. Is that what you need?"

"Indeed, indeed, and yes! I will get screwed!" she hollered.

Brandon abruptly grasped her shoulders. "You need a man's hard cockerel inside you, filling you with his seed? You need a kid?"

"Indeed, damn you! I said as much, didn't I?" Angry and confounded by his scrutinizing, Amelia attempted to disregard him, unexpectedly squinting back tears. "Presently, let go of me!"

Brandon turned her around solidly and pushed her facing her work area, his solid hands squeezing her down. Her enormous cap tumbled off, bobbing to the floor.

Amelia thought back, her eyes wide with shock. "Brandon! What—" He lifted the dress. Slap! Her naked butt stung. He had punished her!

"Hush up! I will give you what you need!" Brandon opened his pants and pulled out his hard cockerel with one hand, wetting the end with saliva. The other hand pushed her solidly down onto the work area. Amelia heaved when she felt his rooster brush against her inward thighs. One finger examined her pussy, at that point two, feeling her, extending her, setting her up. She was as yet smooth from her masturbation.

Brandon guided the top of his cockerel to the passageway of her pussy. A fast push and the crown spread her lips, dwelling inside. Staggered, Amelia snorted as he bumped, pushing his legs between hers, constraining them more extensively separated. Short, hard pushes took him more profoundly with each stroke. Her body acclimated to his essence, reacting to the contact with more grease, facilitating his entrance. Putting two hands on her shoulders, Brandon's hips started enthusiastically slapping against her butt.

Amelia panted from the power of the coupling, her breasts thrashing about, ricocheting against the work area. She got the edge and hung on. Her psyche was inundated with confounded sensation. At that point, her clitoris hit the work area, and her head swam. With every profound drive, his crown brushed the length of her channel, contacting the passageway to her belly. Many a stroke. Again her clitoris hit the work area, and she shouted out as her vision obscured. At the point when she could see once more, Brandon moaned as his hands dropped to her hips, holding her firmly as he ground against her, pushing and examining as profound as possible reach as a great many beats of semen shot into her. It had taken under two minutes.

At the point when his grasp decreased, Amelia took a long breath. More terrible than no coupling for quite a long time was arriving at excitement when the demonstration is unexpectedly finished. With equivalent amounts of outrage and dissatisfaction, Amelia glared behind her. "It is safe to say that you are very done?"

"Goodness, no, Amelia. My cockerel is still hard, and I plan to fill you once more. Presently unwind."

It was valid. She felt no decreasing non-abrasiveness. Shocked, she shut her eyes. The long length of him covered in her sheath filled her so stunningly!

His hands climbed to her shoulders. Amelia strained further. However, his fingers burrowed and pushed, working her shoulders and back. Her section slickened by his discharge and her developing wetness, Brandon started slow, delicate stroking. Before long, his hands moved around to her front, unfastening her dress.

She looked down, watching his hands work. "Very little highlight that, is there?"

"Quiet, lady." He pushed the dress off her shoulders where it clustered about her abdomen.

Amelia neither aided nor blocked him.

Pulling her up, Brandon kissed her neck and snacked her ears, meanwhile testing her pussy with his hard chicken. His kisses went to sucking and nipping.

She felt him moving about behind. A look back, and she saw him pulling off his shirt and opening up his pants further. At that point, he inclined forward, his hands first measuring at that point, pressing her breasts. For long minutes he touched and plied, periodically flicking and moving her areolas.

At last, his contacts brought down to her midsection, at that point her mons. With one hand pressing a breast, the other came to down for her sex, carefully touching her outer lips before brushing her engorged clitoris. Amelia bit her lip to hold back from groaning in delight. It felt so great! Yet, he hadn't asked first, and Amelia was resolved to blame him for that. Stubbornly, his fingers examined and stroked, at times on schedule with his pushing. Joy rose and tempted her. Before she knew it, she whimpered, at that point, whines became heaves, and soon she was shaking her hips, pushing back to meet his pushes to take a greater amount of him inside her, snorting as he skewered into her middle, filling the length of her hole.

Brandon held her nearby as she inclined toward him. Working his cockerel to put it, quick strokes, he changed hands from one breast to another, the other hectically scouring her pleasure community.

Amelia's moans developed. Superbly delectable, she thought.

Detecting her reaction, he expanded the rhythm.

She dropped back to the work area; her consideration zeroed in on his entrance and his finger-play on her clitoris. Her short cries became stronger. As her peak assembled, she squirmed about, pushing against him, the sound of their coupling wet and loud. Unexpectedly she was there. Amelia sucked in a long breath and let out a profound, throaty groan, shaking with rapture. Brandon pushes quicker, increasing her climax.

Having been discharged before, he had the option to keep a high level of delight. As Amelia's breathing eased back, Brandon diminished his speed, examining the length of her.

"You – you didn't cum?" she inquired.

"No, Amelia, the ball was in your court. Try not to stress; I will fill you once more. Presently unwind and appreciate it."

She shut her eyes and dropped her head down to the work area, murmuring as gentle waves of delight jerked through her body.

Long, moderate strokes were joined via touches and kisses to her neck and back. Running his fingernails behind her edges and the sides of her breasts brought serious shivers and sharp breaths in. Brandon shifted his entrance, calculating initial one way. Afterward, another, long lethargic strokes followed by short brisk pushes and afterward pulled her hard to his hips as he pushed profound into her. Meanwhile, his hands wandered her body, touching, scouring, tweaking, tempting.

Amelia reacted with groans and wetness, hungry for additional. Brandon extended his pushing, flexing his butt to give each push additional infiltration. Stretching around, he squeezed the two breasts, crushing them, moving her areolas in his fingers as his cockerel ground into her. She moaned and whimpered, squirming and kicking against his hardness. Amelia snatched the work area, angling her back to give him simpler access.

Before long, Brandon's hips started hammering into her, shaking her, her breasts moving against the finished wood. Her pressing factor building, Amelia heaved on schedule with his lively beating. A hand-wound down her hip, scouring her mons and flicking her clitoris. At the point when she came back once more, her pussy shaking around his cockerel, Amelia tossed back her head and shouted. At that point, two hands held her hips, moving her to and fro as his rooster wounded in and out. A noisy snort and he hammered home, pushing, pushing against her as he held her immovably set up. Somewhere inside her, his crown scoured the mouth of her belly, jerking and regurgitating forward a great many sprays of more semen. Amelia snarled as she shivered, her pussy spasming pleasurably around his pulsating part beating somewhere inside her, creaming her dividers.

Brandon hung over and kissed across her back before pulling out. She, out of nowhere, felt empty, unfilled, powerless. Notwithstanding the work area and him behind her, she would have slid off the work area to the floor. Her butt and thighs were sodden and tacky, dribbling from the combination of ointment and semen. Before long, it would dry and afterward tingle. Hearing him bungle around, she went to see, at that point squinted, doubting. He was taking his boots off! At that point, she gazed suspiciously.

"That is no joke!"

Venturing out of his pants, he climbed behind her, his rooster bouncing.

Amelia attempted to stand and fizzled. "Brandon, I don't figure my legs will take any more–"

"Not an issue," he said. Hanging her arm onto his shoulder, he got her and hauled her around the work area. "We will accomplish something other than what's expected now in any case."

Brandon put her down in the work area, moving between her legs. She watched him, her demeanor indiscernible. He inclined down and kissed her shoulder, touching as he worked his way to her neck. At that point, he moved to the next shoulder, rehashing the kisses and strokes. Tenderly, he measured her huge breasts, feeling their weight. They filled the palms of his hands. Brandon's thumbs went up and flicked her areolas. Coming to down, he licked the underside of one breast, at that point the other, followed the edge of every aureole with his tongue. For long minutes, he focused on them.

Down he kissed and licked, circumnavigating her stomach button, at that point down considerably further. Amelia breathed in, anticipating that he should contact her sex; however, he evaded it, prodding as he lifted a leg and worked his way down to behind her knee. At that point, he went back, licking. When he contacted her zenith, he blew delicately on her red, puffy labia, and she forcefully sucked air. At that point, he started down the other leg.

As he approached her, releasing focus once more, Brandon pulled the seat nearer with his foot and plunked down. Setting her legs onto the arms of the seat, he did light, speculative contacts with his tongue, at that point sink into firmer licking. Amelia shut her eyes and groaned. She could feel his seed spilling out of her pussy. His mouth licked her perfectly, at that point started investigating her swollen, rosy labia; at that point, further into her touchy inward lips. His hands climbed along her sides and began solidly stroking her breasts.

Reacting to his ministrations, she started moving her hips under his tongue, attempting to expand his contact with her clitoris. All around, he surrounded it, lower to plumb her releasing hole, at that point back up again to her swollen clit. To differ the contact, at times, he dropped down to her perineum and rear-ended, licking and sucking meanwhile, before ascending back to her engorged and erect nubbin of joy. Some of the time, he brushed that consuming hard focus of her excitement, not long before dropping down to go to her under lips and drink her nectar. Amelia's groans became whines.

"Goodness, gracious, goodness!" she cried. Without acknowledging it, her legs lifted into the air, her hands holding them separated, opening her sex to him. Brandon's oral considerations brought her higher, and putting her legs behind her elbows, her hands came down to touch his hair and face. As her need ascended at this point higher, she encouraged him with delicate strain to keep in touch.

Reacting to her energy, one of his hands dropped down, and he drove two fingers into her smooth section. Her groans developed, and her hips kicked while his tongue flicked and fingers examined. Building quicker and quicker, he lathed her cut until Amelia abruptly wheezed before letting out a long, low stable. Holding him immovably, crushing her legs around his head, delight, practically agonizing, washed through her, spouting from her pussy.

Brandon ascended and snatched her legs. Pushing them onto his shoulders, he completely mounted her, crotch to crotch, in one stroke. Amelia cried in shock at the unexpected attack. He snatched her shoulders and started a fast, unpleasant beating into her streaming place. Shaking from the power of his pushing, each time pulling out until his rooster lay right inside her, at that point with a hard, wet slap against her crotch, his hardness drove profound, separating her. Amelia snorted, each push filling her, brushing her belly. She curved her back, opening herself to him. At that point, astounding herself, she came back once more. At the point when her brain cleared a piece, his hands dropped to her hips. She understood he should be close. Coming down, she delved her nails into his pistoning hindquarters, pulling him more tightly. One stroke, two, and afterward, he held her immovably, pounding from one side to another, as she felt his cockerel swell and fit somewhere inside. Many sprays filled her once more, and Amelia shook as a more modest climax washed over her.

Brandon took another full breath, gradually allowing her legs to down. Amelia recoiled at how solid they were. He began moving once more, gradually, tenderly.

Amelia put two hands on his chest, shaking her head. "No. No more."

He halted, still within her.

Amelia felt bare, however completely uncovered under his extreme look. "You-you're the first in quite a while. I'm getting sore."

He touched her cheek. Putting his hands all over, he inclined forward to kiss her, yet she dismissed. He glared. "What's wrong, Amelia?"

"No kiss," she said, not taking a gander at him.

"Presently, that is no joke."

"I'm not!" Her head snapped back, green eyes blazing. "No kiss! Not like this!"

"Not along these lines? Do you realize another approach to mate? However, the positions change to create a kid, the man enters the lady and puts his seed inside her pussy." Eyes bolted to hers; he inclined down until his face almost contacted her and murmured, "Am I frightful?"

Frightened, she squinted, at that point, got some distance from his look. "No, Brandon, you're not."

"I gave you what you needed, isn't that right? You even had delight in it. Why not a kiss?"

Amelia confronted him, her voice calm. "I needed to be taken, and you took me, and indeed, you gave me joy. Yet, you didn't ask me first. Kisses are for darlings. We just screwed. Presently let me up."

Brandon took a gander at her searchingly, yet her face was a cover of lack of bias. Dismissing, he gestured, and there was a sucking commotion as he pulled out from her. Assisting her with sitting, he went to a corner table holding a pitcher and bowl. Pouring water, he got a towel, soaked and wrung it, and gave it to Amelia. She grimaced, at that point, hesitantly took it, altogether cleaning her groin, thighs, and tummy. When she was done, he took the towel, flushed it, and cleaned himself.

He looked as she pulled up her dress and re-secured it, at that point changed the band and the little coin tote inside its folds. Three passes of her hands and vague murmuring, and everything about her was once again into the right spot, from the wrinkle of her dress down to the last strand of brushed hair. A weak smell of jasmine exuded from her.

As she recovered her cap, he watched her while getting his tunic into his pants. Brandon made a sound as if to speak. Amelia took a gander at him suspiciously, an uproar of feelings inside her.

"What you say is valid," he said, "I didn't ask you straightforwardly. If it's not too much trouble, trust me when I say I could never intentionally hurt you. You might have said no whenever, and I would have halted." He came to down and pulled on his last boot, tapping the heel to change the coziness. "What happened pesters you. What would you like to do about it?"

"I don't have a clue!" she snapped. "Whatever I — "

All at once, the clock on the mantle tolled—multiple times.

"Ten chimes?" Amelia swore, shaking her finger irately at him. "I should meet Dalinda an hour prior! Until I return, you stay here! Is that reasonable? I don't need you pursuing me or drifting around."

"Indeed, my Lady."

Amelia flung open the entryway with an accident, bursting into the lobby. "Nora? Nora! Where right?"

The youthful, blue-looked-at, blonde guardswoman rushed a few doors down. "Here, Lady!"

Amelia held out her hand. "I'm late, and since I would prefer not to be any later, we're going by wizardry. Give me your hand. Please! Try not to be modest!"

Nora swallowed and gestured.

Amelia immovably got her hand, while the other moved in a hidden example. "Jovahn esh mish kemsa!" And they disappeared with a fly noticeable all around.

* Chapter 3 *

Amelia and Nora showed up on the doorstep of the Whisper Wind house. Defensive spells held her or some other unforeseen visitors back from showing up inside the actual house. Just close family had the advantage of mystically moving straightforwardly into the house. However, the enchantment required was broad and costly, an interaction that anybody with cash or force utilized to keep out intruders – or more awful. Amelia's mom had put comparative charms about her own home here in the capital.

A pale Nora battled with the shocking eventual outcomes of teleportation. Amelia disregarded her and rapped on the passage.

After a second, a gatekeeper opened the entryway. Seeing her, he bowed. "Woman Amelia."

Amelia remembered him yet couldn't remember his name. "I know I'm late. However, I was unavoidably confined. Is Dalinda prepared?"

The watchman shook his head. "The tutor? No, Lady, she left soon after nine ringers. Three family watch went with her."

"Gracious. I see. OK. Is Lady Tia about?"

The gatekeeper looked genuine. "Excuse my assumption, Lady Amelia; however, I should ask, is this a decisive crisis?"

Amelia pressed together with her lips. "Actually, no, not actually. Why?"

"My directions from Captain Hunter were very clear. Crucial crises are the only motivations to intrude on Lady Tia, Lady Mindal, or Lord Reison today. It's simply Marta, the child, and myself disapproving of the front entryway until late this evening. Every other person is on vacation by Lady Tia's express requests. Marta and I are a helpless substitute; however, Tilly, the cook, has left a great deal of arranged food in the kitchen if you wish. I would be glad to head servant for you."

Amelia would not return home as there was an excessive number of inquiries to manage. Nor could she see her mom. Awfully a lot more inquiries there. Tia was her cleric and her companion. At this moment, she required both. Amelia murmured, shaking her head. She would not like to upset her companion's private occasion with her better half. "No, much obliged. Your proposal of accommodation does your Household credit. We're not remaining. Mother's Blessing to you and your family."

"Much thanks to you, Lady. May the Son of Heaven award your solicitation," he smiled, gesturing at her dress and band.

Amelia pinked as she gestured and left, her speed lively.

Nora rushed to make up for a lost time, standing amazed at her paramour's temperament. Ladies who put on the dress and scarf were normally glad, even lively. Her fancy woman didn't appear to be all things considered.

Quickly, they arrived at the edge of the downtown area where advertisers and road sellers were set up. The roads and streets were loaded up with individuals. Provincial ranchers with their late-spring produce, dealers lauding products, uncouth young ladies, bumbling young men, and elegant small kids wending between and about the numerous grown-ups on their business, the poor adjacent to the well off, generally excited for the sights and not a couple of looking for a touch of spare change. Road artists busked adjacent to trinket creators peddling merchandise close to dealers of juice and brew and food—meat on a stick. Dribbling bread patties loaded up with beans, cheddar, and hot flavors—plenty of cakes and great sugar sweets. Scents and commotion and warmth filled the air, and shading was all over.

Some smiled at Amelia and more than one human-made greeting; however, she disregarded them. Amelia expected to notice Dalinda. However, she realized it was a remote possibility. The light of the three suns beats down, turning the air sweltering and close. If lone she'd had something of the tutor, she could utilize the following spell, yet she didn't. A couple of the spells she knew were divinatory. After almost two hours of energetic strolling, Amelia ended, parched. Her unexpected quit is alarming Nora, and they almost impacted.

"Enough of this," Amelia said. "How about we go get a bar and chill for a piece."

"Indeed, Lady." Nora cleaned her forehead, calmed. She had expected an all the more comfortable investigation of the roads. The cloth shirt under her protective chain layer was doused, and an intermittent breeze was deficient to accomplish more than bother. Given a decision, Nora would have worn cowhide, all things being equal, yet her lieutenant had demanded heavier assurance.

Amelia looked about; at that point, she appeared to see her watchman. "I'm grieved. This hasn't been a stupendous task for you, has it? It's likely more than thirty degrees cee at present. My control over the components is fairly restricted, yet perhaps this will help." She signaled rapidly, expressing a curt expression Nora didn't exactly get. Amelia contacted her on the shoulder. The heaviness of the substantial chain was no more.

Frightened, Nora checked to ensure it was still there. "It–it's light! I don't feel it by any stretch of the imagination!"

"I believe that will help. It will go on until tomorrow. Not on par with a super cold beverage, but rather we will cure that insufficiency next in any case. Maybe I ought to ask you for your proposal?"

"My Lady?"

"It doesn't need to be extravagant, simply perfect."

"Indeed, Lady." Nora glanced around. "Indeed, the Black Stallion is close here, however—"

"In any case, what?"

Nora looked despondent. "It's on the opposite side of the obstruction."

Amelia grimaced. "Also, that is an issue?"

The watchman peered down, humiliated. "No, Lady."

"Simply lead the way," she snapped.

As they adjusted the corner onto West Starshine Road, Amelia saw a sign for a public house. Sappho's Fountain was set up in 2087. The sign was newly painted. Beneath it was the male image, crossed out.

Ladies, just, Amelia considered. "Stop. What might be said about that one?" she asked, pointing.

"Not a decent decision, my Lady."

Amelia saw a few ladies enter. "It looks legitimate. Also, it's nearer. We should go."

"No!" Nora got her arm. At the point when Amelia glared, she let go. "Please, Lady. You may get injured."

"I need something to drink, and food is beginning to sound great also. What sort of risk could I be in?"

"It's ladies just," Nora clarified, moving to hinder her further.

"I can see that! Presently we should go!"

The watchman impeded her direction immovably. However, her eyes deceived her vulnerability. "If they let you in, and they presumably, dislike as not, you'll draw in some unacceptable sort of consideration."

Amelia grimaced. "I'm getting genuinely burnt out on my gatekeepers guiding me and intruding in my choices. I'm around two seconds from sending you home."

"Woman, the custom is lesbian or sexually unbiased. Your dress and band advise everybody you're hoping to mate. With men," Nora underscored. "Some may accept it as a joke. However, others may think you were searching for a battle, for sex, or possibly both. Furthermore, they most likely will not take 'no' for an answer."

Amelia gazed vacantly as it sank in. "I see."

"May I talk uninhibitedly, Lady?"

"If it's not too much trouble."

"You don't strike me that way; however, in case you're into the rough stuff, I may know a couple of spots. You know. Safe words, not all that much."

Surprised, she took a gander at the guardswoman nicely. "Possibly later. I barely get enough of the normal activity. In any case, at present, the solitary thing I need within me is cold lager."

Nora grinned, gesturing in the complete arrangement. "Along these lines, my Lady."

* Chapter 4 *

There was a thump on the entryway.

"Come in."

Jaime entered Captain Fisher's office, conveying a plate. "I brought supper up. The cook said you haven't been as the day progressed."

He sat in his seat, gazing out the window. "Take it back."

Jaime set the plate around his work area. "Roberto couldn't hold back to discuss your meaningful discussion with her Ladyship today. It appears he heard certain commotions."

Moving around the work area, she noticed the Purge Knife lying on the work area. With their unmistakable markings and red handles, such bent edges were given to youthful Ba'lorian ladies who endure their Rite of Adulthood by a close family member. Many were exceptionally old. The sole motivation behind the blades was to ceremonially murder an attacker. Up to that point, they were put away safely and were not shown straightforwardly.

"How are you doing this, and what is that doing here?" she requested.

He went to take a gander at her, his face quiet. "Did you realize I had a sister? I did. Melanie. I miss her, Jaime. She didn't endure her Rite, so it passed to me."

Jaime shut the entryway, pulled a seat around the work area, and sat before him. "Brandon, take a gander at me. For what reason is this Purge Knife around your work area? It doesn't have to do with the wrongdoing Duchess, isn't that right? Let's assume it doesn't!"

"That relies upon what she chooses. I don't think it'll end up like that. However, one never knows, isn't that right?"

"You should converse with her! Did you?"

"Indeed and no."

Wariness fought with dread in her face. "What the blasts does that mean? Did you reveal to her you love her?"

"No."

"However, you did engage in sexual relations? I imply that was the—"

"Indeed, we had intercourse."

"Blessed Mother of Rena and God's Great Blue Balls! This is so incredible! You can't reveal to her you love her, yet you experience no difficulty stuffing your cockerel into her!" There was genuinely harmed in her voice. Standing, she got the Purge Knife and shook it at him. "Brandon, she is my brother! On the off chance that she says assault, I must say assistance slaughter you! In a customary manner!" Beaten by ladies of the casualty's House. His name struck from the participation moves of his own family. Maiming and evisceration. She was reviled to meander as a phantom.

Maddened, Jaime spun, kicking a wooden seat so solidly it flew across the floor, colliding with a table against the divider, pushing it over. At that point, she kicked his work area a couple of times before hurling it over, dissipating books, papers, and the supper plate. Dish sets and earthenware production broke with a loud accident. Jaime beat the blade handle against the few times before shaking her clenched hand at him. "Damn you, Brandon! Damn you!" Tears gushed down her face.

Outside, a far-off shout and the sound of boots running nearer could be heard. An interruption, at that point, the entryway burst open. Tamaron Boatswright, blade and knife drawn, ran in. Behind him stood Eleanor Whitestar, examining the room, her Elven longbow drawn with bolt good to go.

Seeing no adversaries, Tamaron delayed, confused by Jaime's pacing and dull glower while his commander sat smoothly among the garbage. Jaime vented with another kick to the toppled work area.

Uncertain, Tamaron made a sound as if to speak. "Everything okay? We heard a commotion."

Brandon gestured. "Individual conversation. I think the most exceedingly awful is finished." He stopped, his eyes narrowing on the sentry. "I thought you should be off this evening."

In the entryway, the mythical being dialed down the draw on her bow and followed, displeased by the bogus alert. Sheathing his weapons, Tamaron shrugged. "Lost a wager. No cash, so I chose to remain nearby. We had that endeavored theft a year ago about this time."

"Great. Please close the entryway on out."

Tamaron looked at his lieutenant, his eyes augmenting at the Purge Knife in her grasp. Jaime frowned at him, at that point, dismissed, cleaning her eyes. Seeing his chief's obscuring look, he snapped a salute. "Indeed, sir."

At the point when they were separated from everyone else once more, she plunked down on the toppled work area, sniffing and scouring her cheeks on her sleeves. "Good, position or no position, you converse with me! Reveal to me all that occurred. What's more, I need everything." Her dull eyes were splendid with torment and outrage.

Brandon murmured. "After you left, I went to the first floor and held back to catch her. I met her. However, I wasn't ready for the truth."

He peered out the window, sunshine quickly blurring to sundown. Light globes in the room were inside simple reach. However, neither one of the ones moved to enact one. Outside, light lighters worked their straightforward sorcery, turning on the streetlamps.

"I guess I ought to have quite recently gone to her quarters after I talked with you," he proceeded. "Who can say for sure? The pointless theory now. In any case, I disclosed to her I needed to converse with her in private, and I wouldn't be put off. She was furious. However, she did as I inquired. God, seeing her in that dress!"

Jaime shook her head. "You don't get it, isn't that right? Her mom is the person who can understand brains, and afterward, just under the right conditions. Amelia is only a lady. She can peruse the unobtrusive prompts men once in a while use, yet you can be very much like a divider, Brandon. She doesn't have the foggiest idea of how you truly feel since you've never advised her. What's more awful, you made me vow not to say anything! Also, the Lawgiver assistance me; I respected it."

Brandon gazed out the window.

Jaime signaled at him. "OK, I'm finished. Go on."

"At the point when she went to go into the workplace, I saw she wasn't wearing clothing. At that point, the smell hit me."

"The smell?"

"At the point when a lady is energized, prepared for coupling. Indeed, it was hard before I understood it. Furthermore, I was at that point furious about her going spots without a gatekeeper. An excursion downtown doesn't care for a little while to her folks. I would be OK with her meeting her folks without one of us alone. The Duchess is a most considerable lady. Girl of Saint Charlotte and more youthful sister to the Queen. A Master of the Northern Star Mages, High Priestess, and like the sovereign herself, a solid psionicist – you know, those individuals who can do things just by pondering them? One of the kindest and most sympathetic ladies I've at any point met, the duchess is likewise one of only a handful few individuals I'd be truly frightened by on the off chance that she at any point lost control with me. At any rate, I revealed to Amelia I didn't need her sneaking off without an escort. She was mad but conceded the point."

Brandon scoured his face with his hands before proceeding. "I think it was desire more than anything. Realizing she was going out to get pregnant. Realizing she needed rearing, that she was prepared for it was beyond what I could stand. Regardless of whether she went out after that, I needed to have her. I purposely caused her to concede what she planned to do, what she needed. At that point, I took her."

"Did she say stop?" Jaime inclined forward, the blade in her grasp held firmly, dreading his next words.

"Indeed, she did. Also, I halted."

Jaime breathed out with help; at that point, she shook her head. "Hang on. I'm confounded. On the off chance that you halted when she said no, did you or didn't you mount her?"

"I was preparing for a fourth coupling when she requested that I stop."

Jaime's eyes broadened. "Fourth? Did you screw her multiple times? I'm almost certain it's been some time for her. A long time at any rate. It's a marvel she could even walk!" Then she smiled. "She should not have been excessively vexed if she let you cream her pussy multiple times. She probably released like a fixture!"

"The point, as she reminded me subsequently, was that I didn't inquire. After I got her to concede what she planned to do, I advised her to hush up because I planned to give her what she needed."

"On the off chance that she was just about as prepared as you say, for what reason didn't you inquire? She probably won't have even gone out!"

Brandon turned away, humiliated. "We were contending. Once more. As you said today, it is by all accounts what we do nowadays. Here and there, I think she takes an opposite direction toward battle. However furious as she might have been, she could have said no, and seeing her, smelling her preparation, the chance of dismissal was beyond what I could stand." He murmured. "I got what I needed, and she got what she needed. However, I sold out her trust simultaneously. What's more, no, I didn't find time to tell her I love her."

"Brandon, you have never given me a motivation behind why you never disclosed to her how you feel. On the off chance that you had, a ton of battling between both of you might have been dodged. Trust me; it hasn't been charming to persevere. In any case, this? This could cost you your life! You will reveal to me why you've kept quiet, and I'm not going to take no for an answer!"

There were a few seconds of quietness before he at last talked. "I guaranteed the Duke I would watch her with my life. He disclosed to me not to exploit her and not to introduce myself as an admirer. Until now, I have kept my statement to him." Brandon glanced through the window, examining the road underneath inactively. "He was correct, as well. I can not adequately ensure her on the off chance that I'm sincerely included. In all actuality, I haven't been making a legitimate showing of it for quite a while. Presently, paying little mind to what Amelia says, it's finished. On the off chance that my assertion merits anything, you'll be her next Guard Captain. You're more than prepared for your order."

"Simply because of your savage preparing. So the Duke picked you? What was your experience before you entered her administration? You have probably been a knight."

"What I advise you is for the wellbeing of companionship. I was a Queen's Arrow."

"What? Did you work for Royal Intelligence? Be that as it may, "

"The Duke made the solicitation, and the Queen decided to respect it. I was suggested and delivered from my past responsibilities." He took a gander at her harshly. "I can't say any longer than that. I gave my vow to the Duke and later gave my allegiance to Amelia by some basic honesty. I should pressure, Jaime, that my past work for the Queen isn't for public information."

Jaime stood up and went to the window, processing his words, Purge Knife still in her hold. "Lawgiver assistance you, Brandon. I'll sound her out first, yet depend on it; I will converse with her Ladyship." She gazed straight toward him. "Also, nothing – I rehash nothing you say will alter my perspective. I'd, in any case, follow you into the haziest pit, yet considering all that you've advised me and all that is occurred, I am not, at this point, limited by any orders you may give me.

"After the entirety of your long periods of administration, you may have moved toward the Duke for delivery from his limitation. Normally, disclosing to her Ladyship why you expected to address the Duke would sabotage your orders. Awful nobody thought to ask her Ladyship her perspectives. Despite her position as the Duke's beneficiary, she's a grown-up and has the privilege to be dealt with as needs are. On the off chance that I was her Ladyship, I'd be painfully pissed once I took in the score. I realize I am. Since tomorrow I may need to execute my companion." She remained to leave, the blade solidly next to her. "Around evening time, I will become inebriated. Goodbye, Brandon."

"Much thanks to you."

She halted at the entryway, declining to pivot, her voice getting. "For what?"

"Your kinship has implied a ton to me, as well."

Jaime grunted as she began cleaning her eyes once more. "If I'd tuned in to insight rather than honor, I'd have told the transgression duchess how you felt quite a while past, or if nothing else moved you into letting it be known. If I'd tuned in to my sentiments, I would have disregarded all that and been inside your bed and had my way with you myself quite a while past. I knew how you felt for her and kept my tranquility. It appears honor ties us both. However, for all the worth I have given to respect, I'm learning it here and there constrains us to act like numbskulls."

She yanked open the entryway and ventured out, yelling in her sleeping shelter voice. "Boatswright! Discover Gault! He's most likely still in the kitchen. Advise that lazy bum to get a brush and tidy up the Captain's office. Fast, tidy up as it were. He can clear more completely for glass tomorrow. Try not to upset the Captain except if he or the transgression Duchess say something else for the remainder of the evening. So far as that is concerned, except if we're enduring an onslaught, don't trouble me. Anything comes up, go see Sergeant Whitestar."

Boatwright looked into the steps, eyes stuck to the blade she held. "Indeed, Ma'am!"

* Chapter 5 *

The Black Stallion Inn was packed. Indeed, even with Nora driving the way, Amelia was grabbed and felt up by a few supporters abruptly, expecting to stand up and move nearby. Several men drifted around, doing their inadequate best to be smooth. The air was thick with cologne.

Amelia waved her hand pretentiously, her eyes squinting in the vapor. "Possibly later, refined men. At present, what I need is a private supper and something to drink."

The admirers moved away, just to be supplanted by different hopefuls.

Exasperated, Amelia mumbled and brushed her dress, and blue changed to green, and the red band blurred to white. Alarmed by her change and the disclosure of otherworldly capacity, they processed about, confounded. Abruptly spying two nubile blue-clad wonders entering the premises, the men disappeared.

The server took their request and got back with an enormous pitcher.

"At long last," Amelia moaned. Amelia and Nora filled their steins and drank generously. The beer was acceptable and super cold.

"They should spend a fortune getting ice," considered Nora.

"Their cooler and cooler are presumably captivated to remain cold. Like at home."

"Truly? It should be straightforward wizardry to do at that point."

"Barely. It took me seven days of serious fixation and projecting for the cooler and one more week. I daresay it would have taken their caster about the equivalent, and he likely charged at any rate 10,000 gold royals for the help." Nora gagged. Amelia proceeded. "I need to apologize for hollering at you prior. You held me back from making a simpleton of myself and most likely a great deal more awful."

Nora hacked, making a sound as if to speak. "It's me—ahem, I must guard you, Lady."

"So I'm told." Amelia inclined forward. "Nora, what's your opinion about me?"

"Woman?"

"Do you trust I'm an individual of my assertion?"

"Uh, indeed, Lady," Nora insisted mindfully, pondering where this was driving.

"I need your assessment, your legitimate examination. Suppose it's not too much trouble. Talk unreservedly. Will you do that?"

Nora cleaned her brow, wanting to be elsewhere. "Indeed, Lady."

"Great. It is safe to say that you are cheerful working for me?"

Alleviated, Nora gestured enthusiastically. " Lady! You treat us well. Great compensation, great food, great quarters. A fantasy ticket, my old sergeant, would say. The Captain and Lieutenant keep me jumping. However, I'm learning more than I could do in the local army. Indeed, Lady, I'm upbeat in your administration."

"Shouldn't something be said about me? Advise me sincerely. If there's something you figure I ought to hear, this would be a happy opportunity to advise me. What's more, if it's tattle, you don't need to tell the source. All good?"

Nora took a gander at her insightfully. "I'm your sword, Lady, and I'll bite the dust to ensure you if need be. I don't feel great about this. However, I'll do it since you need it. I've just been in your administration for a little more than a year. However —you don't appear to be by and large upbeat. It used to trouble me that you and the Captain battle constantly; however, it was disclosed to me, so I approved of it."

"Clarified? Advise me. What precisely would you say you were told?"

"That you and the Captain were either going to slaughter one another or – or …."

"For sure?"

"Mate." Nora couldn't meet her eyes, becoming flushed irately. Screw like crazed hares attempting to repopulate the whole earth was the expression she'd heard. "It—it's not what I said, my Lady, fair, but rather I grew up around ponies, so when I was told different things, it appeared well and good."

Amelia scowled. "Ponies? What are you discussing? What things?"

"That the Captain has been with you quite a while, and you used to be old buddies. I grew up around ponies. My family is herders. Youthful horses in their first warmth. They get particular and disagreeable, hard to oversee, peeing before the steed to show their availability. After the steed gives them what they need, they settle down. They said once both of you sorted it out, you would return to acting naturally, and things would be typical once more."

"I see. What's more, how am I expected to be?"

"Glad, for the most part. Asking your acquittal, Lady, however, the alone time you appear to be cheerful is with your girl. The others say you used to joke and giggle constantly."

Their supper of cold sandwiches and servings of mixed greens showed up. Amelia nonchalantly took a nibble. However, her psyche reeled. It was valid, she understood. It had been quite a while since she snickered.

Nora was excessively anxious yet to accomplish more than squirm with the cutlery.

"You've given me a great deal to consider, so for the time being, you're free. Eat. In case you're as yet hungry after, request more. I know ponies just a bit. Warriors, then again, have consistently been nearby. I have a good thought what amount even a lady fighter can take care of."

The youthful guardswoman began moderate yet completed her dinner and likely arranged a subsequent sandwich.

Amelia tasted her beverage nicely. When Nora at long last drove her plate away, Amelia dropped a gold regal onto the table and held it up. It was commonly what the feast was worth. "How about we go. We may return later; however, at this moment, I need to check a couple of things."

Nora got her protective cap, stuffing the preliminary round of nut bread into her wallet before rushing after her.

Outside, Amelia turned east along the primary lane. A few squares later, Nora was amazed to see they were set out toward the Temple of Osh Mayan, at that point, shrugged, returning her consideration regarding protecting her courtesan.

Under the shadow of the gigantic segments prompting the sanctuary, they wound their way through the constant flow of guests. Once inside, Amelia moved toward the front work area. The air was charmingly cooler and possessed an aroma-like sharp flavor. Following a few minutes, one of the ministers opened up. Gold changed hands, and they ended up in a private chamber.

Before long, a moderately aged minister entered and bowed. "You look for data? Disclose to me everything you can."

Amelia gestured. "There was a youngster I should meet toward the beginning of today. She was focused on an evil mage as of late, and keeping in mind that I don't think anything has occurred, I vowed to pay special mind to her today. A private matter postponed me, and I missed her. I need to know her condition, regardless of whether she's good."

"Her name? Occupation? What would you be able to inform me concerning her?"

"Dalinda Brightburr. Half-Elven. She is a tutor for certain companions of mine."

The cleric murmured and recited while lighting candles and incense. Following a few minutes of request, he calmed. At that point, in a marginally higher, diverse voice, he said, "She is protected this day, her objective accomplished." After a delay, the minister took a full breath and opened his eyes, his tone ordinary indeed. "I trust that addresses your inquiry."

Amelia pulled out her wallet, and choosing two diamonds, offered them to the minister, expressing gratitude toward him. He favored them both and left the room.

"Toward the end, for what reason did he say that?"

Amelia grinned quietly. "At the point when the soul takes him, the cleric frequently doesn't hear what is said. They become a channel for a worker of the god, or even God Himself."

"Gracious. Not something they could utilize only for themselves, I'd envision."

"I surmise not. Since we're here, I expect to get a shower and unwind. Probably the best masseurs in the city are here in this sanctuary."

They made a beeline for the fundamental passageway and followed the signs to the shower houses. As they entered the cavern, a priestess drew closer. Amelia passed her a small bunch of coins, saying, "I need the full treatment. Sauna, shower, knead, the works."

Gesturing, the priestess drove them to a stripping room. Taking the short white robe from an orderly, Amelia reprimanded her gatekeeper. "Please. You, as well."

"Woman?" she squeaked.

"You heard me. The only thing more fun than getting ruined is somebody to impart it to. You at any point had a full treatment previously?"

She shook her head.

"All things considered, at that point, you're going to. Get undressed. Garments in there." Amelia highlighted the open wicker chest.

"Imagine a scenario in which I need to safeguard you. My Lady, Captain Fisher would have my head on the off chance that anything happened to you!"

"We're inside the sanctuary. Unwind, Nora. If anything could get past every one of the charms and the ministers, I question you would make a big deal about a distinction. Presently strip!"

"Would I be able to keep my blade?"

"No weapons past this point," articulated the going to priestess solidly. A few beginners entered the chamber. One gave Amelia a plate on a neckband engraved with numbers, at that point, joined another to complete the chest containing Amelia's shoes, dress, handbag, and sunhat. Coordinating with numbers embellished the wicker chests. Amelia put the jewelry around her neck. Another pair hung tight for the despondent Nora to complete before giving her a comparable robe and neckband.

Once in their robes, the priestess drove them to a close-by sauna. Outside the entryway, they draped their robes on snares. When they entered, a few of the ladies inside looked up, at that point, continued their visiting or shut their eyes in the warmth.

To breathe easy, Amelia got some information about herself, where she was from, where she grew up. Nora,

Amelia learned, was a more youthful girl, brought up toward the east, among the moving slopes of Zashandi close to the beach front city of Portsmouth. Not keen on moving wedded immediately, she had made a trip to the capital and joined with the state army and found that she enjoyed being a hero. With four years of watch insight and her administrator's proposal, she was thinking about the customary armed force when she found out about an opening in Amelia's family monitor.

"From the start, I considered disregarding it, yet my sergeant said you and Captain Fisher had great notorieties. He likewise said the chief would show me things I may never get the opportunity to learn. Furthermore, he has."

Amelia laughed. "Without a doubt? It's ideal to realize I have a decent standing. What kind of things would you say you are learning?"

"Mending, hand to hand fighting, and practice with an assortment of weapons. I'm continually gaining some new useful knowledge. Skipper Fisher is deucedly acceptable with a long blade. He says some are better. However, I've never seen them."

Amelia noticed, "You like Captain Fisher."

"Indeed, Lady."

"Why?"

"May I talk uninhibitedly, my Lady?"

Amelia waved her hand. "Obviously."

"Does this have something to do with earlier today?"

Amelia solidified. "What makes you say that?"

"You were truly furious when we left. You have disclosed to me twice presently it's alright to express my real thoughts, so I will. On the off chance that I make offense, simply advise me and I'll apologize and hush up. Did both of you have another battle?"

"You may say that," Amelia supported.

Nora shook her head tragically. "He's a decent man, the Captain is. He works us hard, yet he's reasonable. Furthermore, you're an extraordinary Lady. I'm glad to serve you. It's wrong that both of you battle constantly. I, without a doubt, trust you get it settled soon."

"I do as well," Amelia said unobtrusively.

"My Lady?"

"It doesn't matter. Come," Amelia said, standing, "how about we go to the shower. You're in for a treat."

Recovering their robes, they left the sauna and finished the signs a few halls to a huge chamber, with the number eleven in enormous numbers outside the entryway. The dividers of the shower were canvassed in a constant undersea fresco. A few seats and a couple of tables of cleaned marble edged the room.

The actual shower was heart-formed, completely three meters wide in the middle and five meters long. A stepping stool with hand rails plummeted into the water on the adjusted finishes, while at the pinnacle, an immense, meter-long erect phallic wellspring overhung the pool's edge. A hefty stream of gurgling water spouted from the crown before spilling into the shower. Scarcely discernable underneath the moving water were implicit seats. The shower could, without much of a stretch, hold twelve individuals. What's more, now and then did.

The fledgling went into the room and bowed. "Will you want orderlies to help you?"

Amelia saw Nora gazing at the tremendous stone phallus and shook her head in delight. The orderly smiled back, and after putting down new towels on a table, let them be.

Hanging up her robe, Amelia slipped into the foamy warm water, settling down with a murmur. At the point when Nora didn't follow her in, she turned upward. "What's wrong? I thought you'd been to showers previously. Also, unquestionably you were here during your Rite of Passage."

"I've been to public showers previously, Lady, however never here. The sanctuary in Portsmouth isn't so exceptionally excellent as this. I have never seen one that percolated to such an extent. For what reason does it do that?"

"Other than the principal source, water from a few different lines keeps the shower full. There are channels close to the top to hold it back from flooding. It is cleaned, warmed, and enhanced with new water. The abundance goes somewhere else. I'm advised it assumed control longer than a year to lay every one of the lines." Amelia loosened up to expand her lightness, appreciating the heated water stroking her body.

Nora stepped in and sat close to Amelia. For a few minutes, they grabbed the cleansers and containers of shampoos and chemicals, washing peacefully, thriving in the warmth. A light breeze from a top vent held the air back from being excessively warm and moist. Amelia utilized a delicate brush on the young lady's back, at that point hung tight. Nora unexpectedly howled.

Amelia glared, turning around to her. "What occurred?"

"Something contacted my thigh. On the opposite side of me."

Amelia laughed. "Ok, you've tracked down the mystery of the sanctuary showers and a significant justification their ubiquity. There are some others also, at various levels. You need to move around to discover them, as they aren't all at similar tallness or even a similar point. Some utilization the critical factor of the planes to knead. Others use them for delight. A couple of stay in until their skin is wrinkled, until they can at this point don't stand, and the orderlies in a real sense need to lift them out."

"What do you mean, Lady?" Nora looked confounded as she cleaned Amelia's back.

"You can utilize the planes to jerk off."

The young lady looked questionable.

Amelia highlighted the opposite side of the pool. "Close to that dolphin mosaic is a decent one. It comes up from the actual seat. Not excessively intense, but rather consistent. A little shaking of your hips is all you need. Several other great ones close to those seahorses over yonder."

"How would you – goodness." She dismissed, her face red.

"Indeed, I've been here previously." Amelia washed off and moved out. Nora rose to follow. However, Amelia shook her head. "You stay. Appreciate this treat. Give it a shot. I will not leave until we're both done, I guarantee. At the point when you are done here, one of the priestesses will carry you to me."

Nora considered dissenting, yet the firm look in her eyes controlled it. She sank gradually once more into the water. "Indeed, Lady."

Amelia got dry and slipped on her robe, at that point deftly wrapped up her long, light hair into a towel.

"Great. Have a ball, Nora. Somebody will be by to mind you later."

Once outside, Amelia peered a few doors down to the enormous divider clock. Almost two ringers. Next to the entryway on the divider was a huge edge, inside which was a huge circle imitating a clock. Little snares were on the hours and half-hours and held two labels, a green one with "start" and a red one with "finish" on it. She moved the red tag from two chimes to three. Specialists getting out and about would let the room be up to that point, yet no more. From experience, she realized they conveyed their count sheets, and more than two hours required a wellbeing check.

She followed the foyer, gesturing to those she passed. Amelia before long went to the focal parlor, an enormous room embellished with all way of sculptures and base-help carvings of stream and sea creatures and wall paintings of the great sea and riverine shores. Overhead, by mirrors, sunlight from outside was coordinated down into the underground room, making it light and bright. Many individuals loose on love seats and cushions, some eating or drinking while they visited. Others just napped or read.

Such as herself, the majority of those present were affluent, and nearly as many were landed respectability also. She knew a significant number of them by name or, if nothing else, notoriety, and the vast majority of them knew her also. Like some private retreat, the unwinding lounge inside the ripeness god's sanctuary was a spot to trade merriments and even business. A ton of exchanges between the Great Houses were led in this very room. The individuals who didn't realize Amelia erroneously imagined that they could handle her for impact at court or favors at home here in the capital. They before long educated in any case.

An older minister moved toward her and bowed. "Woman Amelia, a delight to see you. It's been quite a while."

Amelia radiated in acknowledgment, giving him a brisk embrace. "Father Ramas! I, however, you were in the City of the Suns."

"We go where we're required. How is your visit? Is everything agreeable to you?"

"The help is great, not surprisingly. It's me that is unwell."

A look of concern crossed his face. "Is there anything I may get done for you?"

"No, however, I thank you for the offer."

The minister turned down the volume. "I realize Tia Whisper Wind is your questioner nowadays. She is able; however, some of the time, an outsider is better. I would be glad to hear you out or even discover another cleric if you like."

Amelia gave him a quick kiss on the cheek. "You're caring. Enticing, however, no. A decent body rub seems like what I need at this moment. Is there one accessible?"

Father Ramas grinned. "I'll see what I can do." Pointing to her dried hair, he said, "Maybe somebody to take care of your hair and nails also?"

"Incredible. I have a young woman with me. Her name is Nora, and she's in Bath Eleven. When she is done, will you see that she is brought to me?"

The minister bowed. "Obviously. Like this, please."

The room had two beginners situated around a huge, agreeable seat. Whenever she was situated, one beginner brushed and interlaced her hair while the other went to her fingers and toes. When they were done, she was directed to a second room with an enormous, vigorously assembled, and cushioned table. An attractive, blond minister welcomed her. "Hi, my name is Darby."

"Hi, Darby." Amelia sneaked off her robe and climbed onto the table. With a murmur, she extended and set down onto her tummy. Some place over the rooms, artists played a lazy, wonderful tune; the sounds are floating in from an open vent in the roof.

"Music, alright?"

Amelia gestured.

"Towel?"

"If it's not too much trouble. I'd like a full body rub, Darby."

"Generally excellent," he said, putting a towel for unobtrusiveness over her back.

Amelia permitted herself to completely unwind as he applied the oil and started scouring it into her skin. After he dealt with her back, including some difficult profound muscle work, he worked his way down her thighs and calves, spending long minutes on her feet. When he was back up to her shoulders, she was sleeping.

* Chapter 6 *

The commotion of individuals going into the room brought Amelia unexpectedly conscious. Panting as she sat up, she squinted, at that point, got at the wide sliding down her exposed shoulders, pulling it close. Nora and a youthful priestess stopped in the entryway, amazed at her response.

Darby stood up from his seat. "It's OK, Lady. You just nodded off." He poured her a glass of water and gave it to her.

Amelia took the glass appreciatively, depleting it before talking. "How since quite a while ago did I rest?"

"About 60 minutes. Simply a decent rest is all. It appeared as though you required it, so I put a cover over you and let you rest. I trust that was agreeable?"

"Indeed. Much obliged to you for your thought." Amelia rose from the table.

"My Lady, might you want to complete your back rub?" Darby asked.

Amelia shook her head. "My robe, please. I improve. However, I speculate I'd simply nod off once more. Darby, I'm certain Nora here will make the most of your abilities. Have you at any point had a full body rub, Nora?"

"Uh, indeed, Lady, when I turned into a lady."

"Ok. At your Rite of Adulthood inception in the sanctuary. That was quite a while back. Indeed, you ought to have one at this point. They are great."

Nora gave a slight bow. "I'm overpowered by your liberality, Lady."

"Hogwash. Live it up." To Darby, she said, "I'm returning to the principal space for a beverage. Kindly have her brought to me when you're set."

"Awesome, Lady." Darby gestured as he completed the process of cleaning down the table. He smiled at Nora. "I'm prepared when you are, Miss. Would you like a towel?"

The priestess moved to one side while Amelia left the room; at that point, she pulled the entryway shut and trailed. At the passage of the principal relax, the priestess contacted her arm. "Woman?"

Amelia turned. "Indeed?"

The priestess looks concerned. "Excuse my assumption, yet would you say you are OK?"

Amelia glared. "What makes you believe I'm not?"

"Kindly don't complain. I'm prepared to be a healer, Lady. Your energy air is everywhere. It was wild when you stirred, and afterward, it shrank to barely anything, and now there are flares of orange and red, similar to you are out of equilibrium. You are fretful, similar to you've had an enthusiastic stun. Has something occurred? I can get a guide for you."

"Not all things need to be spoken going to other people!" Amelia snapped, at that point, checked when she saw the alert in the lady's eyes. "My statements of regret. I realize you are simply attempting to help. You're correct. I'm not feeling like myself. I had trusted that some guilty pleasure here in the sanctuary would improve my viewpoint. It has not."

The priestess looked eagerly at Amelia for a couple of seconds, at that point, gestured. "Some consider the sanctuary only a spot for sexual delivery, for amusement, and it tends to be that for the individuals who wish it. Yet, the Son of Heaven is additionally the divine force of mending. Thus we are prepared to give recuperating to the body, yet the brain, the heart, and the soul. Like the Lawgiver, He adores you. At the point when you are prepared, we are here for you, Lady Amelia. Meanwhile, you referenced a longing for something to drink. Mention to me what you wish, and I will be glad to carry it to you."

Amelia dealt with a little grin. "A berry spritzer would be pleasant. Much thanks to you."

She returned the focal parlor and moved close to the divider, away from different bunches of guests. Choosing an enormous, over-stuffed seat away from the others, she subsided into it. Court interests were the exact opposite thing she needed to persevere. Hearing some development close by, she shut her eyes to pretend rest.

Amelia was frightened to feel the texture against her skin. She gazed upward. It was the youthful priestess, once more, covering her with a cover.

"Your beverage is there on the table. If you need to rest, there is no spot better than God's House. The seat is agreeable to sit in, yet it's not intended for relaxing rest. We do have private places that can offer better rest, Lady Amelia." To highlight the point, the ice in the glass clunked as it moved.

Amelia shook her head. "No, much obliged. I'll simply trust that Nora will wrap up."

"As you wish." The priestess inclined down, delicately kissed her cheek, and favored her, at that point disappeared.

Briefly, Amelia had felt like she was being gotten into bed by her mom. At that point, she nestled into the seat and shut her eyes. Unyieldingly, her psyche dashed back to the occasions of the morning. For quite a long time, she had been anticipating the prospects and delighted the Solstice occasion had guaranteed. She didn't know Dalinda very well, yet as her conjugal applicants had all demonstrated ailing somehow, so she hosted expected a wild and unbridled get-together following quite a while of progressively incensing forlornness. Masturbation and toys gave some delivery. However, the genuine delight of coupling was in the joining, the offering to another individual, regardless of whether that sharing just desired.

Her brain floated back to when Brandon had taken her. He had felt better, his solid arms holding her nearby, the vibe of his hard part pushing into her. More than once, that delight had topped to climax with him inside. However, the way that he had controlled her, taking her without straightforwardly asking heretofore disturbed her, bothering pride and feeling of legitimacy. The more she considered the big picture, the more it annoyed her. More than once, Brandon had saved her life, and he focused on her and Dalyanni. As of not long ago, they had managed everything well enough that she had considered less him as her gatekeeper and more as her capable and reliable companion. However, even as things had some way or another soured between them, the giggling less successive. Still, he was there for her this previous winter, solid and supportive, with a word of wisdom when Dalyanni shouted in her fever. She likewise realized that after their long journey in the colder time of year storm, he had permitted others to go to him solely after she and her little girl had been focused on.

Amelia swept back a tear. He had taken her without her authorization. However, she hadn't revealed to him no. At any rate, not from the start. She might have executed him with a motion and a solitary expression of force, yet that idea never had at any point entered her brain.

Accusing him of assault filled her with awfulness. On the off chance that she charged him, she was certain he would not deny it. At times Brandon was so irritatingly honor-driven she figured he would have been more qualified as a paladin, a hero in support of the congregation.

As the person in question, by sacred law, the proportion of his discipline was her decision if she charged him. In any case, it had become custom to distribute demise, and the crucial factor for those of the Great Houses to correct passing was significantly more serious. She'd seen it previously – the bloodlust in the essences of the ladies keen on getting retribution and their blood-spread faces and drenched apparel after that.

Amelia drove the recollections from her brain. It was too simple to even think about seeing them coming for him. Realizing she would be the reason for his demise was a lot to bear. In any event, when they were throwing angry words at one another, Brandon had been there, giving solid counsel, shielding her and her little girl from risk. No, she was unable to charge him. However, she additionally realized that the occasions of the day had perpetually changed their relationship. In any event, she would need to excuse him. He had crossed limits and double-crossed her trust. The possibility of him being gone from her life was excruciating. Transforming her face into the pads of the enormous seat, she unobtrusively sobbed until rest by and by guaranteed her.

* Chapter 7 *

"Escort?"

Indeed, Amelia shot upstanding, panting, glancing about in disarray. At that point, she saw Nora and a youthful priestess taking a gander at her oddly.

Nora was bewildered. For a vacation expected to be loaded up with fun and skip around, the wrongdoing Duchess didn't seem, by all accounts, to be living it up. Or maybe the inverse. All the more along these lines, the tear streaks on her kohl eyeliner showed she had sobbed well into the night. Nora made a stride nearer. "Woman, is everything OK?"

"I'm OK," she addressed harshly. "A terrible dream. Nothing to worry over."

The priestess remaining close to Nora gave Amelia a soggy towel, at that point, ventured back consciously. At the point when Amelia looked perplexed, the priestess highlighted her own eyes, and appreciation unfolded. Amelia energetically cleaned her face, cleaning endlessly all hints of the kohl and lipstick, thankful for the second to gather her contemplations. Seeing they watched her, she rehashed, "I'm fine. Truly."

The priestess gestured, gave Nora a consoling pat, at that point left.

Nora hunched down to eye-level before talking unobtrusively. "Do you wish to get back, Lady?"

"No! Aren't you making some great memories?" Amelia went after her somewhat alcoholic spritzer, the glass clammy from ice since a long time ago softened. Taking a full breath, she brought down the vast majority of it in one go, at that point, slowly inhaled before completing it. Resolved to change the subject, she put down the glass and smiled at Nora. "You were away for quite a while. Did you make some great memories?"

Nora stood up, gazing at close-by furniture, pink flushing her ears. "Indeed, Lady. He was most .. satisfying."

Amelia smiled. "Superb. Presently, how about we go do some shopping."

* Chapter 8 *

At The Dragon's Lair, an upscale hotel on the city's western side, they at long last settled down for a delayed supper. Nora was overpowered, contemplating whether she was not out of her profundity. After a little nibble outside the sanctuary, they had gone consistent for almost five hours, from one shop to another, occasionally strolling, now and again leasing a gig, entering places obliging the well off. Pretty much every spot visited yielded products to the transgression

Duchess, and a while later, the businesspeople had kindly consented to convey the buys. Nora was utilized to serious wheeling and dealing – for garments, for food on the lookout, and if she didn't wrangle, she had the right to pay whatever the traders charged. Wheeling and dealing were something aristocrats didn't do. Her number-related abilities were barely enough to make do with, yet Nora was certain the all-out uses surpassed what her family had acquired in the previous ten years! The youthful guardswoman was starting to see exactly how much cash her manager had. However, for all that, she could see that the transgression Duchess was as yet despondent. Indeed, even supper appeared to not affect.

"What's wrong, Nora? Don't you like the feast?"

Nora turned, surprised. "No, Lady. The food is acceptable."

Amelia stopped mindfully. "It has been a difficult day. Maybe you'd prefer to be diminished?"

"Indeed, Lady. That is to say, no, Lady."

Amelia caused a commotion.

"That is to say. Indeed, it's been a taxing day," Nora clarified, "In any case, I am fine, Lady. A lot of this, I am not used to, however, except if you are disappointed with me, I am regarded to serve and secure you."

Amelia flickered, at that point, grinned. "Message understood. While this is less secure than the sanctuary, there are twelve equipped watchmen inside a brief distance, attentively covered up, to shield visitors and prevent any difficulty from turning crazy. I'm certain about your capacities, Nora. The reality you are as yet in my administration past your first year implies that you have some ability and have incredible potential. If you decided to leave, for reasons unknown," and Amelia lifted her hand to stop her dissent, "I would prefer not to lose you. However, I would be glad to compose a letter of suggestion. Your Lieutenant compliments you, and I confide in the judgment of my officials. You previously saved me once today from a tough spot, demonstrating to me both your legitimacy and their evaluation. I'm sorry you're not happy with these environmental factors. Indeed, I had seen that, as well. Be that as it may, today, I need you to be something beyond my guardswoman. You don't need to say or do anything extraordinary. Simply be with me. Would you be able?"

Nora gestured.

Amelia breathed out. "Great. Attempt a portion of the jellied currants. Furthermore, mint dressing is acceptable, as well. Here, have some more chicken in plum sauce."

After twelve courses, obediently inspecting everyone put before her, the youthful guardswoman could scarcely move. The transgression Duchess as far as it matters for her, ate generously, yet never apparently completing one plate moving to the following. Toward the supper's finish, they went into a parlor to unwind, tasting wine while artists played relieving, calm tunes. Nora discovered the overstuffed seat to be agreeable. To an extreme thus, for the following thing she knew, the transgression Duchess was remaining over her, tapping her on the arm. Getting up with a beginning, she sat up. "My Lady? Something incorrectly?"

"No. I'm exhausted with this. I'm going to the gaming tables."

Nora gestured, rapidly cleaning her eyes clear as she rushed behind, scolding herself for nodding off. Up the steps and through a lobby to another parlor. More brilliantly lit and noisier than the music relaxes, there was an assortment of card, dice, and wheel games to be seen. There were effectively 100 individuals in the room, with scores of workers handling about with a plate of drink and food. Preposterous, Nora heard the town ringers ringing. NOON! No big surprise, she was worn out. With a moan, she followed intently behind her special lady.

Amelia scoured the room, searching for the main thing to stand out for her.

"Woman Amelia! A delight!" A blond man in a short white silk robe drew closer, trailed by a couple of intensely built guards.

Amelia turned, gesturing in acknowledgment. "Pericles. How are you?"

The Hellene gave a bow that was some way or another affable and disparaging simultaneously. "Goodness, much better since you are here. It is consistently a delight to see you, Lady Amelia. We've missed you! It's been a total of months since your last visit!"

While he talked, he tenderly guided Amelia to an unfilled table. Amelia, as far as it matters for her, let him. Nora limited her eyes dubiously at his touch, drifting inside arm's scope. His watchmen floated directly behind her. On the off chance that they attempted to get among her and her fancy woman, they would discover exactly the amount she had taken in the previous year!

"Pardon me. Woman Amelia, is this one yours?" Pericles shouted as he pulled out a seat for the transgression Duchess.

"Indeed, she is."

"Exceptional. Where have you been concealing her? However, somewhat harsh around the edges with some cosmetics and a visit to the salon, she would be pleasant. It is safe to say that she is free or bondswoman?"

"She's promised her administration to me. However, she's her lady. I don't bargain in slaves. You realize that, Pericles."

"Pity. All things considered, if you at any point alter your perspective, I'm certain I could accomplish something with her." Nora took a moment's aversion to the man.

Pericles inclined near Amelia. "What's your pleasure this evening, Lady?"

Amelia waved her hand over the tabletop, giving up a few pearls. "Dice, first."

Without an adjustment in disposition, Pericles scooped the jewels up as deftly as they had shown up. "Generally excellent. I'll be back with your chips. Would you care for anything to satiate your thirst? A few pieces to entice your range?"

"House juice."

"On the double, Lady Amelia."

As Pericles left, a few workers removed the table, supplanting it with one intended for dice tossing. As seats were brought and a vendor set up, different benefactors meandered over. Pericles returned, trailed by an insufficiently clad chestnut-haired and earthy colored peered toward Hellenic young lady bearing a plate with a heap of betting chips and an enormous, clear glass stein loaded up with a golden fluid.

"Here are your chips," Pericles said. "Cleo has been appointed to you, Lady Amelia."

Cleo setting the stein before Amelia, bowed, at that point, ventured back.

"If you need anything, anything by any stretch of the imagination," he proceeded, "just advise her, and she will take care of it on the double. Except if you'd incline toward male organization this evening?" A grimace crossed Amelia's face, and he bowed with a twist. "My Lady, as you wish."

Amelia gathered the dice from the seller, and stood up, put a few chips onto a square, and afterward tossed the dice. Amelia won the first round, lost the following two, and afterward won the following four. She had Cleo request some foods grown from the ground for Nora and more house juice for herself, giving Cleo five chips for installment.

As Cleo moved past, Nora halted her. "What amount is that?" she requested, highlighting one of the chips.

"Ten royals," Cleo replied and afterward was gone.

Ten gold royals each! Each chip was a month's wages. In the city, the beverage would have cost six or seven coppers! Nora's head felt light. So the main engraved on the chip implied ten. Those with more than two were 25. At that point, Nora looked once more. A pile of chips with 100 set apart on them. The wrongdoing

Duchess had more on the table than she had gone throughout the day. As the dice and betting kept on rolling, the guardswoman stressed, apprehensive if the wrongdoing Duchess lost such a whole, what it would mean for her family.

Regardless, the products of the soil espresso were valued when they came. Nora hadn't understood how hungry she'd become. What's more, after a taxing day, espresso was what she required. Both were before long gone.

The wrongdoing Duchess, consumed in her game, scarcely contacted the beverage, keeping up a constant flow of talk with the vendor and different players. As the minutes ticked by, Nora watched Lady Amelia's heap of chips develop at an idle, however consistent speed. Twice, the table vendor was changed, with no impact. Amelia unexpectedly passed the dice to another in the next hour, got her beverage, and moved off. Nora rushed to get up to speed to her fancy woman, leaving the surprised Cleo to bounce up and hysterically gather the chips before following them.

Amelia scoured the room. Seeing a table with open seats on one of the raised floors, she headed over. In any event, Nora was directly behind her, giving a couple of pushes with the applicable statements of regret to hold back from getting isolated. Up the steps to the arrival they went.

There were two tables. One was full. However, there were three void seats at the subsequent one. Amelia gestured to the players. "Is this seat accessible?"

The two moderately aged men gestured, half-grins gleaming across their appearances. Amelia knew them both. The clean-cut man was Dominic Iscarios, a well-off Hellene shipper and part-proprietor of the nearby office of the Mercury Lines exchanging organization. With a military hair style, the subsequent man was Thorvald Moonhart, a local army official and a wealthy respectable. Both had played against Amelia before, and however they had each won a portion of the games, Amelia ensured that when she won, it was worth more. The three more youthful men were finished outsiders, with no undeniable familial similarity to both of the more seasoned men.

The three more youthful ones straightforwardly assessed Amelia. The nearest, a young with a meager mustache, slapped his knee, saying, "Here, pretty thing!"

Amelia overlooked him. Taking a gander at the two more established men, she asked, "What's the game?"

"Three Rivers poker," addressed Thorvald. Two cards down, four cards up, and one card down, and the best five checked.

Amelia gestured and plunked down in a vacant seat.

The subsequent young fellow, a blonde, who had a minimal measure of chips before him, saw the platter of chips Cleo set close to her and protested. "That is an excessive amount to begin in with."

Amelia took a quick look around. Dominic gestured, and Thorvald just shrugged. She had presumably, however much every one of them consolidated. "All good. Nora?"

The youthful guardswoman ventured forward. "My Lady?"

"Find a comfortable place to sit," she taught. Going to the others, "You wouldn't fret, isn't that right?" Amelia generally partitioned the chips into half without sitting tight for an answer, moving one stack to the unfilled seat on her opposite side.

"My Lady?"

"You realize how to play a game of cards, isn't that so? Great. Plunk down. These chips are yours. Give a valiant effort, even against me, do you hear?"

"How might I watch ?"

Amelia gave her a hard gaze, and Nora plunked down. She pondered exactly how Captain Fisher would deal with her when he discovered, and she had most likely that he would. Doing as she was offered, she gulped anxiously.

Amelia took a modest bunch of chips. "Cleo, drinks for everybody. Whatever they had previously. Nora, remove your cap and unwind." As Cleo left with their orders, Amelia grinned expansively at the vendor. "Next hand, new deck, please, and bargain us in."

The hand-finished inside a couple of moments. At the point when a foot under the table contacted within her calf, Amelia said nothing. She considered everything and asked why it disturbed her so. She had come to town for coupling. Regardless, she moved her leg away. At the point when the foot followed, she moaned and sat back, mumbling a couple of subtle words similarly as the foot pushed up between her thighs. Out of nowhere, the youthful mustached man howled and hopped up, banging the table, almost turning it over. "Something messed with me!"

"Possibly it went where it should go," Amelia grinned briskly.

Iscarios and Moonhart took a gander at Amelia and afterward the youngster. Thorvald shook his head. "Plunk down, Gaius, or say goodbye. Also, be adequate to keep up your best possible behavior. This is Lady Amelia, not one of the young house ladies."

Iscarios put down his cards and connected with the more youthful man. However, Gaius shook him off, scowling at Amelia. "You–you magicked me!"

Nora, acknowledging what more likely than not occurred, ascended, her face purpling with outrage, however, Amelia put her hand on her arm, and she hesitantly sat down. Amelia put a heap of chips into the bet, disregarding him.

"What are you?" he requested. "Some fence witch?" The other two young fellows watched, pausing. Dominic dismissed, shocked.

Thorvald held up. "She is a Lady. Maintain your best possible behavior!"

One of the young fellows attempted to ignore it. "She's simply one more virus bitch, Gaius. Try not to allow her to get to you."

Amelia gazed at them wickedly. "You are discourteous young fellows. I expect your sakes; we never meet again." With that, she depleted her glass and held up. Nora rose alongside her, thinking about the amount of a mark her head protector would make several countenances.

Behind Amelia, Pericles climbed the steps, trailed by his two ever-present watchmen. Cleo drifted around behind. Pericles reviewed the table harshly. "Is there inconvenience, Lady Amelia?"

"I thought there was an open spot at this table. It appears I was mixed up." Amelia moved past him and energetically plummeted to the primary floor, Nora quickly behind her. On the floor, Amelia heard a lady shouting toward her. "Woman Amelia! Woman Amelia, hang tight for me, please!"

Amelia halted and turned, her face sullen.

Cleo rushed up, her face arguing. "Please, Lady, don't be angry with my Lord Pericles. He–he needs to talk with you, to apologize for any bother you encountered."

"You should take care of me this evening, right?"

"Indeed, Lady." Cleo brought down her head, eyes deflected. "Order me."

Amelia contacted the thick silver groups on Cleo's arm. To Amelia, they should be iron. Slave. "Discover me a room, Cleo. I need to turn it in."

"Without a moment's delay, Lady. Shouldn't something be said about my – "

"Tell your Master that I'm not angry with him or with you besides. I'm finished gaming for the evening. What I need presently is a bed. Concerning you, I will require your administrations for the remainder of the evening."

"At without a moment's delay, Lady." Cleo apprehensively moved around to lead while not showing up excessively intense. "Along these lines, please."

In another piece of the hotel, Cleo carried them to a two-room loft. Different workers before long followed, bringing new organic products, wine, and glasses. One conveyed an enormous fan. However, Amelia tersely excused him.

A brief timeframe later, Pericles himself showed up, an aide behind him. "Woman Amelia. I've been made mindful of the graceless treatment you got on account of a portion of different visitors. I guarantee you, they have been removed from the premises."

"Iscarios and Moonhart had nothing to do with it," Amelia said. "What's more, Moonhart acted respectably."

Pericles gestured. "So the vendor advised me. Is there something else I can give? Would you care for a masseuse? An extraordinary wine? Undergarments? Anything by any means?"

A worker conveying a plate loaded with chips moved to put the plate down on a table.

"Stand by," Amelia called to the worker. He looked into it, amazed. "Bring that here," she requested.

"It's for the most part present, I guarantee you," Pericles said.

Moving to the table, Amelia took a pile of chips and put them in a safe spot. "On the off chance that I questioned it, I could never return. You are a shark, Pericles. However, you have consistently been straightforward with me. These are for this evening's visit. The rest, take and convert them to diamonds and coin, the last to be close to 10%, less your bonus for cash changing."

"At that point, you will not remain after tomorrow?"

"I will return, however, not immediately. I have other businesses requiring my consideration, some of it away from the capital. I wish to keep Cleo with me around the evening time. Presently, on the off chance that you'll pardon me, I'm prepared to resign." Amelia was too bothered to even think about sitting.

Pericles motioned to the worker, and the plate of chips was diverted. "Your Ladyship. I'm upbeat you are so satisfied with her."

Amelia tightened her lips, gazing at him.

Pericles bowed, at that point, snapped his fingers. At the sound, the workers hurried out. Pericles and his gatekeepers followed them out, shutting the entryways as they left.

Cleo hustled just a bit to Amelia when they were gone, pushed her shoulder lashes down, exposing her young breasts, at that point, set to slackening her belt.

"Stop, Cleo."

"Woman?" She froze a look of dread all over.

Amelia stroked her jaw mindfully, gradually strolling around the young lady. "Nora, did I see a couch in the external room? Indeed? Great. Cleo, do you know who I am?"

"You are Lady Amelia."

"Is that all?"

Cleo dropped to her knees, head down. "If I have irritated you, Lady, if it's not too much trouble, advise me."

"Get up," Amelia said unobtrusively. "You thought you were resting with me, didn't you?"

Standing up gradually, she gestured.

"How could you become a slave, Cleo?" Amelia motioned for her to cover herself.

"My-my folks were poor, Lady." Nervous and confounded, Cleo did as she was offered.

"How old would you say you are?"

"Sixteen, Lady." She shuddered.

"Where are you from? Also, when did you become a slave?" The Kingdom of Tildor debilitates the importation of slaves. However, it permitted it because their laws permitted subjugation for significant wrongdoings like homicide. By law, notwithstanding, following five years, weregild, or the option to get one's opportunity, must be permitted, and no criminal bond at any point endured longer than twenty. Ba'lorian law carefully disallowed subjugating youngsters, and that law was implemented all through the realm of Tildor. It very well may be hard to authorize; however, a Ba'lorian slave could even decline sexual courtesies.

"From Malganna, in the Caloren States. I was seven, Lady." Seeing the expression all over, she hurried to add, "My present expert just bought me the previous summer."

Her answer didn't influence Amelia. On the off chance that Pericles had bought and brought her into Tildor before her fourteenth year, he would be intensely fined, and Chloe would be liberated. It was clear she had been instructed on what to say. Amelia went to Nora. "Take a cushion from my bed and a cover into the other room, please."

While Nora complied, Amelia delicately stroked the young lady's cheek. "I need you to go in the other room and get a decent night's rest. At the point when I need you, Nora will animate you."

"Indeed, Lady." Flustered, the young lady left to the external condo.

A couple of moments later, Nora returned, shutting the mediating entryway. Amelia emptied the water into an enormous bowl, spread out a towel onto the covered floor, at that point, ventured out of her short dress. "What do you think, Nora?"

"Woman?"

"Chloe. Do you figure she would utilize her opportunity?"

"I don't have a clue, Lady."

Amelia hung over a wash bowl, talking as she soaped herself from face to groin, at that point washed off with a wet towel. "If she is acceptable, I might want to take care of her. Consider it. To be taken from your folks as a youngster. If we had lived in her country, it might have happened to both of us. A few groups don't see ladies or young ladies as profoundly as our kin do. Maybe she worked in a huge family? There are scars on her back, yet somebody's gone to the difficulty of eliminating the majority of the proof. Most likely because it impeded her excellence, I don't think she was in a house of ill-repute, else she would act all the more secure with herself. Now and again, I wish I had my mom's capacity to understand individuals." She cleaned down her legs and feet, at that point, started drying herself with a subsequent towel. "I'm asking your assessment, Nora. An aspect of your responsibilities is to survey individuals. Evaluate her."

"I've recently met her. I barely figure I can make such a judgment, my Lady."

Amelia scowled. "Try not to attempt that with me. I've been around officers and patrols for my entire life. My dad valued people who can think and react quickly. You're here because... since ..." Because Captain Fisher – Brandon – thought she was sufficient. She dismissed. "Simply consider the big picture, okay?"

"My Lady, may I know why you need this? It would help me comprehend."

Amelia cleaned her eyes and turned around. "My folks instructed me that administering is a genuine obligation. Some of the time, I tuned in while they examined and settled on troublesome choices. My dad once disclosed that with such countless individuals under our consideration, the sad truth is that there is continually going to be foul play, neediness, and disgust, regardless of the amount we attempt and battle against it. We should do all that we can so the dominant part will succeed and that their lives will be as protected as possible make them. Concerning the individuals who come into our way, we can and ought to intercede straightforwardly. Have an effect where we can. You know. Secure the powerless and defenseless."

"Citing sacred text, and living it, as well." Nora gestured insightfully.

"Not however much I ought to be. Simply something I gained from my mom. Again and again."

Nora grinned at the basic cherished memory. "Guardians can do that." She glanced around and gathered up a cover. "I'll rest here," she said, highlighting the foot of the bed.

Amelia drank a glass of cool water, at that point, climbed bare into bed. "Try not to be senseless. The couch is adequately long. Move it if you should, yet don't rest on the floor. I would prefer not to stumble on you on the off chance that I need to rise later. There's a real restroom, not a bedpan, behind that screen. It's supernatural, similar to the ones we have at home." With a rush of her hand and an expression of force, three lights went out, leaving just the light by the entryway lit.

Nora did her latrine, washed her face and hands, at that point moved the couch. Moving the light nearby, she put it out, at that point, pulled the light cover over herself. She was worn out and more than prepared to close her eyes.

"Nora? Is it safe to say that you won't eliminate your defensive chain layer or even remove your boots?"

"No, my Lady. I'm on the job, regardless of whether I'm resting."

"Very well at that point. Goodbye."

"Rest soundly, my Lady."

* Chapter 9 *

At some point around first light, Nora heard low cries coming from the bed as she turned over. Quickly ready, she moved discreetly. As her boots hit the floor, her sword murmured free. Nora searched for anything strange in obscurity. However, she could make just ambiguously make out the wrongdoing duchess and little else. She went to the light, venturing into her wallet for matches.

"No! Try not to execute him!" Amelia sat up and shouted.

Nora sheathed her sword and hurried over. "Woman Amelia! Is it accurate to say that you are alright? Woman!"

"No! Stop it, please! Stop!"

Nora got her by the shoulders, shaking her. "Wake up! Wake up!"

Amelia stopped, gasped, at that point imploded and covered her face, crying.

Chloe beat on the entryway. "Hello! What's going on?" came her suppressed voice. "I heard a shout. On the off chance that if I don't find a solution, I–I'll get someone! I will!"

Nora took a gander at Amelia, at that point, went to the entryway and opened it. Chloe remained there, earthy-colored eyes tremendous, the light shaking in her grasp.

"It's OK," Nora said, taking the light from her. "I think it was only a bad dream. Get some warm wine for her. I'll leave the entryway opened."

Chloe attempted to peer past. Muted wails came from the most distant side of the dull room.

"Hello!" Nora yelped. "I provided you a request. Get to it!"

The young lady bounced, at that point, catapulted. Nora shut the entryway and returned to the transgression duchess, putting the light down onto a close around evening time stand. The transgression Duchess cried into her cushion. Nora stood a moment significantly, at that point intuitively did how she had helped her more youthful kin, not such countless years sooner. She plunked down, brought Amelia into her arms, and started to shake, stroking her back. "It's OK. Simply an awful dream. It's OK. No doubt about it."

Amelia clung to her, her wails before long calming to battered breathing loaded up with wheezes.

A brief timeframe later, Chloe returned, tentatively going into the room with a decanter and an enormous cup. "Is it true that she is good?"

"I'm alright, Chloe," came Amelia's stifled voice. She sniffed and sat up. Chloe passed her a hand towel. Amelia took it, cleaned her eyes, and afterward cleaned out her nose. "Much thanks to you."

The young lady filled the cup, the steam obvious as its fruity fragrance filled the air. Hands shaking, she got it and drawn nearer. Nora caught the cup and took a beverage before giving it over. "Taste's fine. Be cautious," she prompted. "It's really hot."

Amelia took a gander at them both before taking it from the guardswoman's hand.

"Go on. Truth be told," Nora said. "Get it down. It'll help."

Chloe made a sound as if to speak. "Woman? May I make you something else?"

Amelia shook her head. "No, much obliged. I'm sorry I woke you. Return to rest now."

Chloe bowed, getting the subsequent light, and left, shutting the entryway behind her.

Nora stood up, taking the cup from Amelia. "Another cup?"

"No. I'll be fine at this point." She cleaned out her nose once more.

"Indeed, Lady." Nora put down the cup, at that point, returned to the couch.

"Nora?"

The guardswoman fixed her cover. "Woman?"

"If it's not too much trouble, come into bed with me. At present, I truly should be held."

Understanding crossed her face. Like her more youthful kin. "Obviously."

"Above all, I demand you remove your networking mail. The blade can remain nearby, however not in the bed." Amelia peered down. "Boots, as well."

Nora laughed. "Indeed, Lady." She pulled off her over-shirt, and the chain followed, laying them on the couch. Numerous pounds lighter, she eliminated her boots and big cowhide pants also. She set her scabbarded long blade inclining toward the nightstand. Wearing an undershirt and undies, Nora moved into bed. Amelia moved back, preparing for her.

"Would you like to discuss it?"

Amelia shut her eyes momentarily. "No."

The falter in Amelia's voice gave Nora all the guidance she required. Drawing her nearby once more, she kissed the highest point of her head. "Shhh. That is no joke."

Amelia shut her eyes, crouching close. The light from the light glimmered, projecting wild shadows across the dividers, yet it was soothing regardless. In the far distance, Nora heard the town ringer tolling. Five chimes. Almost first light. Before long, they were both sleeping.

* Chapter 10 *

It was the sound of individuals going into the room that woke Nora. Snatching her sword, she carried up and squatted protectively. The workers peered toward her anxiously yet proceeded with their obligations. Amelia sat close by at another table. Nora stood up, chagrined at finding such countless individuals in the room without thinking about it first.

One worker, with a truck, put down a covered plate before Amelia, at that point another at a second, void seat. Others got an enormous tub, while behind them, a line of carters got cans of steaming boiling water, emptying the substance into the tub.

"Unwind," Amelia told Nora. "Utilize the latrine, wash up, and afterward come have some morning meal." A worker uncovered Amelia's plate with a twist and ventured back. Amelia looked at Nora. "You may wish to dress while that is no joke." Another worker poured glasses of juice, water, and cold milk. Amelia sniffed thankfully. "It smells pleasant."

Nora squinted, at that point, did as she was offered. Rushing through her morning latrine, she washed immediately, at that point, put on her pants. At the point when she got her chain protection, Amelia scolded her.

"Please, Nora, plunk down and eat before it gets cold. Chloe, go get your morning meal; at that point, educate your Master that I wish for him to go to me."

The youthful slave-young lady bowed and left.

Nora lifted her arms and let the weighty reinforcement slide down. A move of her shoulders and a pull assisted it with sitting serenely. "My Lady, individuals are traveling every which way. How might I ensure you if something goes awry?"

Amelia grinned faintly. "Be guaranteed that correct now there are insurances set up. Thus, if it's not too much trouble, sit and eat."

Workers kept on entering, filling the tub. When one worker moved to place oils and scents into the water, Amelia motioned him over. Sniffing through the choice, she said, "Roses, crocus, and violets. Kemetic kyaphi, yes? I suspected as much. I like roses. However, they disagree with me. Gee that is jasmine? Indeed, that and the almond oil. Stop. Some like an alternate aroma for various pieces of the body. I think such a large number of fragrances confound the nursery. Leave a few towels. My watchman will go to my shower."

The worker bowed and went along. When the waterline was reached, the tub was covered to keep the warmth in as far as might be feasible. After the remainder of the workers left the room, Amelia stood up, uncovered, and ventured into the water.

At the point when Nora rose, Amelia said, "Sit. Finish your morning meal. At the point when I'm prepared for your assistance with my hair and back, I'll let you know."

"Indeed, Lady."

"Call me Amelia. At any rate, when we're in private, OK?" Reaching for a cleanser, she started washing up.

"Woman?"

"You've procured it. You're reliable and view your work appropriately. I like that." Amelia washed up her shoulders and breasts. "More than that, Nora, you were there the previous evening for me." She grinned, more to herself than to the youthful guardswoman. "I'd likewise prefer to imagine that we can be companions.

In the years ahead, I will require companions, individuals I can rely on."

"For when you acquire the duchy?"

Amelia gestured, satisfied at the knowledge.

Nora filled her plate a subsequent time. "Woman? That is to say, Amelia? I'm respected for the advantage you have given me. May I pose an individual inquiry? In case I'm excessively forward, advise me, and I'll quiet down."

Amelia limited her eyes, gesturing circumspectly. "Go on."

"I heard you were the third offspring of Duke Thorband and Duchess Dianne. For what reason are your senior sibs not to acquire?"

Breathing a murmur of alleviation, Amelia washed off her shoulders. "My more seasoned sister, Talí Theláyna, loves sorcery. She will not surrender it, declining to have youngsters or even a darling for the time it would detract from her examinations. It was every one of my folks could do to persuade her to fill in as Lord High Wizard for the duchy, to lessen a portion of the obligations from my mom." Amelia sat up on her knees, washed her stomach, groin, and thighs. "My sibling, Moril Marcusha is a good fighter and – indeed, suppose there were numerous meaningful conversations with the tribe chiefs. Moril will become Lord High Marshal when our present one resigns or is executed. So left me. I might have rejected, obviously, and the House bosses would have picked another beneficiary for the Queen to affirm. Like my sister, I love magic and what it can do. We get that from our mom, I assume. However, my dad, indeed, he asked me, and I was unable to disclose to him no." Amelia plunked down in the water and started flushing off. "In case you're done, I'm prepared for you to do my hair and back."

Nora cleaned her hands, at that point, moved over, pulling up a stool. "Which one do I use?"

Amelia highlighted a taller container. "That is the cleanser."

As she washed up the hair, Nora inclined nearer. "You should adore your dad a ton."

Shutting her eyes in delight, Amelia murmured. "Indeed, I guess I do."

At the point when she was done, Nora gave Amelia a towel for her hair. As Amelia stood, the guardswoman took a bigger body towel and started scouring her dry. Amelia gave her an interesting grin, going after the towel. "Nora, I can do that without anyone's help."

Abruptly humiliated, the young lady ventured back. "Ahem. Sorry."

"That is OK. I appreciated the spoiling you gave me. However, I don't anticipate that you should be my body worker. Mother never truly loved the thought, and I surmise my grandparents were that way, as well. Presently that I'm more seasoned, I can value their reasons, yet at that point, I thought it was real trouble." Amelia dried her back and front.

"Did you at any point meet your grandparents?"

"A couple of times, however, I was exceptionally little. After Grandfather passed on, Grandmother Charlotte kicked the bucket the following year. They say she pined away from melancholy. I trust it." Amelia ventured out and dried her legs and thighs. "From that point forward, Grandmother Shara got together and vanished. The story is that my aunties, Queen Dorothy and Princess Theodonra, have heard from her throughout the long term. However, almost no of what has occurred here since has contacted me."

"There are bits of gossip that your Grandmother, Saint Shara, has passed on. Provided that this is true, I reach out to you my sympathies."

Amelia gestured. "It's actual. She slaughtered, fighting against the dim mythical people underneath the destroyed city of Oaken Hill. You recall the seismic tremors the previous spring that shook us here so seriously? I, as of late, discovered that that was the point at which she passed on. Obliterated one of their dull mythical person realms at the expense of her own life." When she saw Nora's premium, she laughed. "I just know a touch of it, third hand or more regrettable. My mom knows more. Maybe when we visit the City of the Suns once more, I'll ask and ensure you're around to tune in to every one of the subtleties."

Nora squinted. "Truly? That is somewhat you – "

There was a thump at the entryway. Amelia rushed into clothing, bra, and a cautious sun dress, as Nora moved to the entryway, calling out, "Who right?"

"Pericles, to see Lady Amelia."

Nora inclined near the entryway, talking uproariously. "Her Ladyship is simply completing her shower. She asks your absolution and to kindly stand by one minute longer."

Alarmed, Amelia halted. "Generally excellent, Nora," she murmured. "Utilize your drive, very much as you did. Simply be certain that you don't submit me to anything without my say as much when you do represent me. OK?"

The guardswoman bowed her head. "Indeed, my Lady."

Amelia added a story-length skirt, slid into certain shoes, and situated herself back at the table. Removing the towel in her hair, she took a gander at a mirror and glared. With a progression of signals and expressions that Nora couldn't hear, Amelia's hair fixed and orchestrated itself in a convoluted course of action of meshes and contorts. "OK, you can give them access."

Nora opened the entryway and stood aside. Their host entered, trailed by his two huge shadows.

"Pericles! So great of you to come. If it's not too much trouble, plunk down." Amelia grinned. Pericles was faultlessly dressed, not surprisingly, yet Amelia presumed he'd had less rest than she when all is said and done; she presented herself with a glass of hot tea, and with the ascent of her eyebrows and a slant of her head, inquired as to whether he needed to join her.

He shook his head. "You mentioned that I come to see you. How may I help the messenger and beneficiary to the City of the Suns?"

Amelia saw his gatekeepers. "You may resign to another room. Nora, kindly go with them."

His watchmen took a gander at Pericles. He gave a brief gesture, and they discreetly left Nora behind them. At the point when the entryway was shut, Pericles plunked down and collapsed his arms, pausing.

Amelia snacked at a cut of toast and took a beverage. "I'd prefer to talk honestly with you."

"My Lady."

"I have looked into the government assistance of the young woman you so sympathetically accommodated me. That was pleasantly done, coincidentally. I could offer to get her for an incredible whole, and the following time I visit, have one more youthful slave introduced to me. I'm exceptionally well off. However, it appears to me there is another option. The advantage to you is that it costs you just time and some benevolence. I'm willing to give the virtual coin."

Interested, Pericles raised an eyebrow. "What kind of course of action would you say you are discussing?"

"Manumit her. I'll pay the expenses for that: the court charges, prosecutor expenses, inking. I'll even take care of the expense of your buy-in in addition to 20%. Have her instructed to peruse, compose, and figure. However much she is keen on. If you like, you may utilize the educational plans of a Hellene prostitute. Reasoning, verse, dramatization, whatever you figure your clients would appreciate examining. If she can dominate it, she ought to learn accounts also. I'll pay her wages and her mentoring costs. At whatever point I visit, I'll hope to see her. I will likewise organize it so that if she turns out to be sick or harmed, she can be taken to my congregation for recuperating. Consequently, you give her food, housing, and dress, and you can anticipate 66% of a day's work from her. Feed her a proper eating regimen, with a decent segment of meat in any event once per day, with at any rate one entire day away from work seven days, and I'll consider it genuinely done. Toward the finish of a year, we'll both choose if we will proceed with the plan."

"Your offer is tempting. I esteem your support at my foundation, regardless of whether you generally appear to leave somewhat more extravagant because you draw in other rich clients. In any case, for what reason would it be advisable for me to do this?"

Amelia gestured. "A proper inquiry. I think she is a jewel in the unpleasant. She acted in any event when she was scared, and she showed different qualities that I prize in my staff. Treat her with generosity just as order, and urge her to learn. Try not to drive her to utilize her body except if she needs to. I figure she will shock you. On the off chance that she doesn't gain good headway, or if, toward the finish of two years, you're not happy with her, I will bring her into my family and pay you an extra 1,000 royals for your difficulty. How might you lose?"

Pericles tapped his finger on the table while he thoroughly considered her proposition. A respite, and afterward, he gestured. "I need this record as a hard copy. No offense, Lady, yet imagine a scenario where something ought to happen to you. I would require evidence for your family if I somehow happened to lay any guarantee against your legacy."

Amelia gave a rude gesture. With straightforward prestidigitation, she waved one hand around another and introduced a look to him.

Pericles grinned, at that point, went after it. Examining rapidly through it, he saw the seal in wax at the base and gestured in understanding. "All that you said, effectively in ink. A man who believes reimbursement of a betting obligation is a dolt. Nonetheless, you have consistently paid your obligations and kept your assertion with me. I will believe this agreement won't be changed mysteriously." He got up and headed toward a side table. Taking a plume, he opened an inkpot, scratched his mark on the report, and threw the plume onto the table. "As an indication of trust on your part, I might want a portion of the wages and the manumission charges in advance."

"That is worthy. On the off chance that you can have the coin and pearls brought from the previous evening, I will give the cash at this moment." Amelia gently tasted her tea.

Pericles went to the entryway and flung it open. "Pythas! Get Chloe and bring her here. Craterous, accompany me. My Lady." A bow to Amelia before he left.

Nora shut the way to the external loft, at that point entered, and shut the way to the internal condo before ensuring everything was OK, a demonstration not lost on Amelia.

Amelia topped off Nora's cup and her own. "Drink your tea. In a couple of hours, we'll be home. At the point when we arrive, you can have the remainder of the day away from work. I'll clear it with your officials. That ought to permit you to rest up after all the going around I've gotten you through."

"There's no need, Lady. I can carry out my normal responsibility when I return."

Amelia looked at her. "It's difficult for you to consider me your companion, right?"

Hesitantly, Nora gestured. "There is a great bay between us, Lady. You are destined to manage, and I am destined to serve. I'm content with that."

"I'm not expecting for us to turn out to be dearest companions. This is new for the two of us. However, I realize that I like you. Kinship sets aside an effort to develop appropriately. You've seen me when I was scared and feeble; at this point, you console me. Indeed, even now, you talk uninhibitedly, a lot more liberated than before we began this experience. Give it a possibility. Give me a possibility."

There was a thump at the entryway. Amelia turned. "Come!"

Pythias opened the entryway. "Woman, here is Chloe." He cleared out for her to pass, at that point, left.

Chloe bowed, saying nothing, sitting tight for guidance.

"Nora, consider what I said." Turning to their visitor, Amelia said, "Chloe, find a comfortable place to sit and sit down, please."

There was one more thump at the entryway. Nora got up to respond to it, and Pericles entered, trailed by his subsequent gatekeeper, Craterous, the last conveying two packs of coins and pearls. Amelia demonstrated that Nora should take the more modest one. From the bigger, she checked out 2,000 royals, scarcely affecting the abundance contained in that. Pericles gathered up the cash while Chloe, her head bowed, watched with misgiving.

Amelia inclined forward to the young lady. "Chloe? A few things in your day-to-day existence are going to change. If it's not too much trouble, listen cautiously to what exactly I'm going to say."

* Chapter 11 *

Outside the hotel, a gig pulled up. It was almost ten chimes, yet the air was at that point thick with heat. Regardless of that, Amelia wore a more moderate, burgundy sun dress with a wide, gold belt. Nora had moved to stay up with the driver. However, Amelia rapped her seat immovably, demonstrating she should ride adjacent to her. At the point when the guardswoman subsided into place, Amelia called up to the driver, "Ten-ten Snapdragon, please."

As they left the midtown region, Amelia looked forward. Seeing her hardened stance, Nora sat discreetly. Around them whirled scores of celebration attendees, appreciating the sweltering summer day and the occasion environment. At virtually every corner, artists busked, and merchants employed their products. As they left the lane and turned onto Snapdragon Street, Nora acknowledged Amelia was shaking. She grasped Amelia's hand. "Woman?"

Amelia held her hand immovably, shaking her head, rejecting eye to eye connection.

Before long, the pony and carriage pulled up before a huge, three-story corner house. The Whisper Wind house.

Nora paid the driver and dropped, at that point helped Amelia down. "Will I have the driver pause?" she asked. Amelia again shook her head. Waving off the gig, Nora moved toward the entryway and rapped the knocker multiple times.

A gatekeeper replied, not quite the same as the other day. "Indeed?"

Nora declared, "Woman Amelia to see Mother Tia, straightaway. It involves some desperation."

He looked at Amelia, at that point gestured, opening the entryway wide. "Come inside, Lady Amelia, and be gladly received." Turning to another watchman, he said, "Eshan, ensure her Ladyship is agreeable while I go illuminate Mother Tia."

Eshan offered a seat, food, and drink, all of which Amelia declined. Like Amelia's own home, the air inside the Whisper Wind home was perceptibly cooler inside, rewarding to having a mage inside the family. Nora utilized her arm to wipe her brow, sweating as much from the temperature adjustment as the warmth they had quite recently left. They remained in an enormous room, loaded up with a line of a few tables and long seats. With its roof vaulting up to the third floor, the enormous room worked as the fundamental eating lobby. To the privilege was a way to an exercise center. To one side was the military quarters. At the furthest finish of the room, the left lobby prompted the kitchen while the correct prompted an enormous family room. Inverse the main entryways was the way to the study hall just as a flight of stairs driving higher up.

The homeroom entryway opened. Out came a young lady of normal tallness and bronze-earthy colored shading, mid-length dark hair and dim eyes, wearing plain tan robes, and exceptionally pregnant. Tia Whisper Wind. To Nora, she seemed to be her age, yet she'd heard from her lieutenant that while the priestess was human, she was a lot more seasoned than she showed up. The gatekeeper reappeared in the principal corridor behind Tia, shutting the study hall entryway before getting back to his post by the front passageway. Nora chose a close-by seat to stand by.

Tia grinned expansively, holding out her arms in hello. "Amelia! It has been for a little while, hasn't it? Be gladly received and disclose to me how you are!"

Amelia decently flew into her arms, embracing her firmly.

Tia embraced her back, shocked by the power of Amelia's grasp. Before long, Tia broke the hug tenderly, yet solidly. Measuring her hands around Amelia's face, she looked profoundly at her before talking. "How about we go talk in private, will we?"

Amelia just gestured, tears spilling uninhibitedly.

Tia guided her toward the flight of stairs. Turning her head, she stopped to call out toward the family room. "Reison? Mindal? The kids are chipping away at some mathematical tasks at this moment. Lessa can assist with the amendments. At the point when they are done, they can deal with their ventures. On the off chance that two or three hours, they need another thing to do, have the more experienced ones work with the new youngsters on retaining the various letters in order, presenting them together in little gatherings, and to work on thinking of them for in any event 60 minutes. From that point onward, they can have some additional rec center time. No more school after lunch today. Good?"

Reison ventured from the family room into the entrance, taking a gander at Amelia with a combination of interest and concern. Mandal remained behind him, her hand on his shoulder. "Is everything good?"

"We'll be up in the church. Except if it's truly earnest, Husband, kindly don't upset us. Would you be able to assist in the homeroom? Much thanks to you. You are a dear." Tia gave Amelia her cloth, at that point inclined toward her arm. "Please, how about we go. That is a young lady."

They rose the steps to the mezzanine level, at that point, took the main entryway on the right, going into the house sanctuary. Tia guided Amelia to an agreeable love seat along the back divider when the entryway was shut, plunking down close to her. One hand started a standard touching of Amelia's back, stroking tenderly.

In the wake of allowing Amelia a few minutes to quiet down, Tia discreetly asked, "Do you have the capacity for talking?"

Amelia burst into tears once more. "I'm so confounded, Tia! I don't need him to pass on, yet I don't what else to do!"

"Need who to bite the dust, dear? Why not beginning toward the start? That is typically best. Take as much time as is needed, and advise me even the littlest subtleties that come to you. OK?"

Gradually, in fits and starts, Amelia started. As she talked more, her voice steadied, and when she completed her story, she was made once more.

Tia kissed her cheek, at that point, embraced her firmly. "No big surprise you're disturbed. I'm sorry I wasn't accessible yesterday for you. Amelia, for something like this, it truly is a crisis. Do you get it? Presently I will pose you a few inquiries and answer as honestly and totally as you can. A portion of these I can think about how you feel, yet I need to ask them for the wellbeing of legitimacy. One has been upsetting you as of now. It's the most significant, yet we should check whether we can defuse it, OK? Great. Amelia, would you like to accuse Brandon of assault?"

Amelia withered, however, shook her head vivaciously.

"Considering your response to the fantasy about him being projected out and his custom passing, I didn't think so. Okay. How long have you known Brandon?"

"Ten years."

"My, my. Only a couple of years longer than we've known each, right? Ten years. How could he become your skipper?"

"My dad introduced him and suggested I bring him into my administration. So I did."

"So your dad got an opportunity to audit his character, and no uncertainty, so did your mom."

Amelia looked astounded. "Indeed, I assume so. I hadn't considered the big picture, yet you're likely correct. However, I don't perceive why it would matter."

"They would need to ensure he was a decent man. He was chosen to ensure their youngster. Up until yesterday, have you had any motivation to be disappointed with him?"

Amelia turned away. "His administration has been model. More than once, he's saved my life, taking injuries implied for me. He's truly adept at ensuring me. Be that as it may, - indeed, of late, we haven't been getting along."

"How about we have some chamomile tea." After some exertion, Tia got up and pulled a line by the entryway. "Or then again, maybe something different?"

Amelia shook her head. "Nothing at present."

Tia shifted her head and saw her, pausing.

"Okay," Amelia said finally, a little grin pulling her face. "I'll have some tea with you."

"Great." Tia gave her shoulder a concise crush before cautiously plunking down once more. "I think attempting to get here, and there is my most un-main thing from being pregnant: that, and the steady tension on the bladder. I simply need to pee constantly! Enough about me. In this way, both of you have been experiencing issues. How long has this been going on?"

"I don't know."

"Recollect. There's been a change going on between both of you. It very well may be useful to know when it started. Likewise, what sort of issues precisely would you say you are having?"

Amelia paused for a minute or two and scoured her sanctuaries. "I don't have a clue. I get it's been ... it's been longer than a year at this point. What do we quarrel over? That is the thing that's so odd. They aren't big things. However, when we're shouting at one another, they appear to be significant. Subsequently, I feel embarrassed the battling got so insane. More often than not, it's simply that he needs to associate with me any place I go or to know where I am constantly. In any event, when I'm home."

"He is your watchman commander. He must know where you are to ensure you. If that is the thing that's annoying you, you're in for a ton of hopelessness when you acquire the duchy. After so long in your administration, I would have thought you were utilized to him watching you."

Amelia shook her head. "I've been around monitors for my entire life. Furthermore, for the greater part of his administration, I didn't have a solitary grievance. It's in things I can't nail down. Like what he looks like at me."

Tia brought her hands into her own. "On the off chance that he was only a renewed person, I'd say supplant him. However, he's most certainly not. Also, that is the thing that's disturbing you. He's your skipper, yet after such countless years and shared difficulties, he's become your companion."

Amelia gestured.

"Do you confide in him?"

She shrugged.

Tia looked at her. "You don't know? That says a great deal, Amelia. You truly need to supplant him on the off chance that you don't know whether you can confide in him. Do you figure he will be perilous?"

"No. How he converses with me, I feel like – all things considered, I feel like a terrible youngster getting shouted at. The disturbing part is that I've never seen him speak more loudly to any other person."

"Fascinating. How's he been with your little girl?"

Amelia cleaned her eyes, turning away. "Dalyanni. He's been just glorious with her. They ramble, and since her

10th-year function this spring, he's been giving her self-preservation preparing, as well." Amelia grinned with humiliation. "At any rate, she's abandoned, needing your significant other to be her dad. No, she adores Brandon, nearly venerating him. If I thought she was peril from him, leaving my administration would be the most unimportant part of his issues. No, I would confide in Brandon to ensure her with his life. Tia, what am I going to do?"

Tia grinned, pressing her hands. "OK. We should change the subject to a smidgen. On the off chance that I review, you began searching for marriage accomplices some time prior. When was that?"

Amelia shrugged. "Last April or May, I think."

"Thus, a little more than a year at that point?" There was a concise thump at the entryway. Tia called out, "Enter."

Jo Mason, Tia's chaperon, opened the entryway, giving Amelia a grin and a gesture on seeing her. "You called, Mother?"

"Chamomile tea, please. What's more, a few sandwiches and organic product also. Much thanks to you, Jo."

"Unquestionably, Mother." The young lady bowed and shut the entryway once more.

At the point when Tia turned around, Amelia was somewhere down in idea. Tia continued her inquiries. "As I review, you were keen on a few neighborhood men of their word. Alunder Tamaron Trader, for one. Ipi Hap-Hathor was another, I accept, and a third whose name I can't remember "

"Moril Tomas Wheelwright."

"Indeed, Wheelwright. Indeed, I'm happy you didn't seek after Hap-Hathor. I've met him, and I don't believe he's an exceptionally decent man. In any case, you never truly disclosed to me why nothing happened to the next two."

Becoming flushed, Amelia peered down. "They revealed to me they weren't intrigued."

"Truly? That is to say, on the off chance that it was valid, for what reason didn't they reveal to you straight away? This is bewildering, so how about we analyze this further. Your mom is drop-dead perfect – Amelia, she truly is, and you acquired a ton of her elegance and excellence. You can redden, yet it's actual. Presently the sorcery may have put them off, yet most non-spellcasters either have an exaggerated thought of what sort of force is included, or they accept they can handle it by controlling you. Be that as it may, they needed to have thought about it. You don't stay quiet about it. Indeed, even without magic to make you more youthful, which you approach, you're as yet youthful enough to have more youngsters. At that point, there's the cash. You're rich and beneficiary to the City of the Sun's Duchy. Youth, excellence, cash, and force. Amelia, you're an opportunist's wet dream. Men ought to be falling all over you."

Amelia gazed at her.

"I realize you would prefer not to share a spouse, and I can't fault you there," Tia grinned. "A lady who has more than one spouse definitely should have the drive important to keep them glad, and for certain men, that would be a full-time vocation in itself. With your enchantment research requests and your developing political association, I'd figure more than one man would destroy you. There ought to be lines of single admirers restless to court to you."

Amelia muttered something.

"Sorry?"

"Not if somebody was debilitating them."

Tia shifted her head. "Presently, for what reason do you say that?"

"Your sister, Judge Tanner, disclosed to me that Brandon broke Trader's sculpture. It was worth very much cash. However, he was reluctant to look for a case with me straightforwardly, so he went to the Queen. So it hit me up indirectly. I paid for the sculpture, obviously, and afterward made a couple of requests of my own. Brandon had disclosed to Trader that if at any time made me miserable, he would hurt him."

Tia caused a commotion. "So you think he made comparative alerts to different admirers?"

Amelia gestured. "That is the reason I went to my mom recently. I requested that she attempt to discover somebody less inclined to be impacted by my over-defensive gatekeeper skipper. I discovered that a large portion of them was more intrigued by my cash and propelling their flunkies. I'm not against a political marriage if it ends up like that; however, if there's no affection, I need to, at any rate, regard him. Else, I'm apprehensive I would before long hold him in scorn."

"Some may say Brandon is only a committed worker paying special mind to his courtesan. Like a brother securing a sister. Before yesterday, would you say you were two at any point private?"

"No."

"Have you at any point needed him?"

"Indeed, quite a while past," Amelia conceded. "The initial not many years together, when we were adventuring, there were a couple of times when I was excessively wiped out or harmed to get us home. Each time, he dealt with me. He is solid and has numerous gifts and abilities. If he had made the offer–and I needed him to!– I would have given myself uninhibitedly. I implied my advantage a few times, yet he acted as he didn't take note. Since he works for me, it wouldn't have been suitable for me to recommend him straightforwardly."

Tia gestured. "Social disparities. I disagree with them, yet there you are. Advise me once more. When you said for him to stop, he did, didn't he?"

"Indeed."

"No contention?"

"None," Amelia affirmed.

Tia gestured. "Obviously, by at that point, he'd as of now climaxed multiple times, so one could contend that by then, he no motivation to compel the issue. The coupling gave you delight, as well, yes? More than once, I review your saying. Since you didn't utter a word, it may appear to his family that you gave an unsaid endorsement of what he did. You don't feel that way; else, you wouldn't be so grieved now. Amelia, I think he discovers you appealing and alluring. Multiple times? Trust me when I say, if there's no sorcery included, that it's quite surprising. No big surprise you were getting sore! Whatever his purposes behind turning you down prior, Brandon presently discovers you attractive. Regardless, you can't allow him to stay as your chief. Do you need him to leave?"

Amelia moaned. "I can't envision him not being near. That is the thing that harms to such an extent. Yet, I surmise I'll need to."

Tia gestured. "Attempt to respond to the following inquiry without considering everything. Say the primary thing that flies into your head. You can't have him as your chief since he crossed a limit. Do you love him?"

"Indeed, I . . . goodness, God. I don't, isn't that right?"

"I think you addressed genuinely. So why have you been battling? Inside a brief timeframe of your knowing him, you discovered him alluring; you needed him. Since you figured he wasn't intrigued, you started looking somewhere else. Brandon, for some obscure explanation, overlooked your advances; however, when you as of late started seeking, he was attacking your endeavors. Your disappointment fabricates, and because you figured he wasn't intrigued, you have been battling with him to get his advantage. You were most likely not even mindful of it on a conscious level. You're scowling. You disagree?"

Amelia frowned at the floor, ears pink. "No. Another person said something very similar to me just yesterday, utilizing an earthier relationship. Go on." Frisky horses in heat.

"You discover Brandon alluring, and he's been your companion for quite a long time." Tia reclined, scouring her gravid stomach. "You know that I was hitched beforehand. Well before you were conceived, my dear. An unfortunate encounter. The contrasts between my first spouse and Reason are night and day. I like and regard Reason personally, and in any event, when I'm furious with him, he approaches me with deference consequently and as an equivalent. He's not simply my sweetheart; he's additionally my dearest companion. Only one out of every odd companion will make a decent mate, Amelia. Be that as it may if you pick a mate with whom you can likewise be companions, indeed, trust me when I say they are the ones to have."

Amelia hit the sofa with her clenched hand. "Why? Why, on the off chance that he adores me, for what reason hasn't he at any point said anything to me? For what reason didn't he just come out and say it?"

There was a thump at the entryway.

"That, my dear Amelia, is a generally excellent inquiry. At the point when you return home, you ask him. No, I can get up. You stay." Tia hungover and gradually pulled herself up. "You're looking more settled. I think you have a few things settled, yes? That is acceptable." She stopped at the entryway before giving Jo access. "We should have some lunch and discussion around a couple of more things, and afterward, I will set you a few undertakings before you defy him."

* Chapter 12 *

Nora paused while Amelia went through almost two hours conversing with the priestess. When they descended the steps together, Nora thought Amelia looked much better, settled and in charge of herself again – and strangely, bothered. Yet, her agony and disarray had been facilitated. Nora affirmed.

Instead of hanging tight for a driver, Amelia demanded they head back home. She expected to think, she said. The half-hour walk passed peacefully.

Sergeant Eleanor Whitestar welcomed them at the entryway. "Welcome home, Lady Amelia. We have missed you."

Amelia welcomed the mythical being housekeeper heartily. "Much thanks to you, Eleanor. Where are my officials?"

"The Lieutenant is in the rec center, rehearsing her sword drill, Lady. Chief Fisher has been in his office since the previous morning."

"Eleanor, I'm going to my quarters. If it's not too much trouble, ask my cousin Jaime to come to me. Nora, before you head off, kindly go to me."

Amelia stepped energetically down the corridor and up the steps. Strangely, it seemed like she had been away for quite a long time. Was it just yesterday that this all started? She pondered. Habitually, she stopped to check the mystical wards outside her room. None of them had been upset. She flung the entryway open, going to her bureau and full-length reflect. The dress from the motel was sufficiently pleasant, she thought, yet she had paid Pericles multiple times its actual worth. The cost of accommodation, she assumed.

Nora stood by calmly a few speeds behind her.

Amelia saw her in the mirror and turned. "You have the sacks of coin and jewels I gave you today? Great. Set them on the bed." When Nora unlimbered her pack and spread them out, Amelia took the more modest one and gave it to Nora. "This is for you."

"Woman?" Nora was dazed.

"Consider it a reward. You've taken in a ton about me, and when I was feeling truly helpless, you console me. That implies a ton. You can go through the cash, part with it, accomplish something for every one of that kin you outlined for me, contribute it, or even set it aside for your retirement. Do whatever you wish. You can even take the cash and strike out all alone on the off chance that you need. In any case, you should realize that I need you to remain."

"I gave you my promise vow as a liberated individual, Lady," she replied, at that point squirmed.

Amelia practically snickered. "Nora, since you've been loosed, I can see that holding you back from expressing your genuine thoughts will be an irritated preliminary for you. Mention to me you're opinion."

"On the off chance that you go through such a lot of cash, will not you go belly up? I like you, Lady; however, I'm concerned that you will devastate yourself with such liberality. If you become poor, how will we respond?"

Amelia was satisfied. "I value your anxiety. Notwithstanding, I won the more modest sack the previous evening at the tables. The bigger sack is the change for the diamonds I introduced. Concerning my riches, I guarantee you that I have bounty more where that came from. A large number of my initial experiences in my dad's interest were—will we say?—productive. What's more, I have grounds and business property. Furthermore, recall about what I informed you regarding administering."

Unexpected knowledge streaked in Nora's eyes. "You are accomplishing for me since you know me. I'm in your immediate circle. Very much like you helped Chloe."

"Precisely. Except if you have different inquiries, you should get tidied up, eat a hot supper, and get some rest. I'll disclose to Lieutenant Starshine you are off the clock until tomorrow."

Nora saluted. "Woman." Hefting the pack, she radiated cheerfully as she left.

Very quickly, there was a thump at the entryway. Amelia moaned. "Come!"

Jaime Starshine entered, shutting the entryway behind her. "Woman, you called me?"

Amelia headed toward the dresser and got a brush. Pulling out the hair fasten, she started brushing out her long blonde braids. "Indeed, Jaime, I did. Pull up a chair, please."

Jaime headed toward a stuffed seat and plunked down, flushed and sweating from her efforts in the exercise center. "How did Nora do, Lady?"

Amelia looked at her in the mirror, her hand brushing out her hair immovably. "She did well overall. At your soonest opportunity, begin giving her official preparation. I likewise need you to enroll a normal entourage of troops. A force's worth. Two organizations of infantry, one of toxophilite, and two soldiers of medium pony. I'll get you the gold in the following not many days."

Jaime looked astounded. "Woman? We don't have space to house them here. Furthermore, will not the Queen be concerned you are raising such a power, particularly here in the capital?"

"Tia Whisper Wind revealed to me that the woody mythical people consumed Athens three evenings prior."

Jaime was staggered. The City of the Suns was a big city of more than 40,000 individuals, further down the Crescent River, joined by the River Seine. On the southeast bank of the Seine was the Christian city of Saint Petersburg, with almost 10,000 people. The little Hellene fishing town of Athens, adjoining the backwoods on the southwest side, had numbered not exactly 1,000. "Since the time our kin came here, the woody mythical people have been our partners," Jaime said. "Do you figure war will come? What's more, do you figure Whitestar will leave?"

Amelia put down the brush and turned around. "I would like to think not, to both of your inquiries. However, on the off chance that war comes, I need to be prepared to get back to the City of the Sun's straightaway."

Jaime gestured, ascending from the seat. "Great, Lady Amelia. Something else?"

"Nora is to have the remainder of the vacation day. From that point onward, she can get back to whatever plan you consider fit. There's nothing more to it."

Amelia got back to the dresser and opened her corrective case.

"Shouldn't something be said about Captain Fisher, Lady?"

"Shouldn't something be said about him?" Amelia immediately applied kohl eyeliner; at that point, she went after the lipstick.

"Hehe mentioned to me what occurred, Lady."

Amelia twirled around, her face dim with wrath. "What? Has he been boasting about it?"

Jaime put her hands up in a fight. "No, Lady! I needed to drive it out of him. I guarantee you, neither of us said anything to anybody. Not that it would have done any great."

Amelia put her hands on her hips; her eyes are limited. "Exactly what do you mean by that?"

"Roberto, Lady. He discussed the clamors he heard when you and the chief ...."

"I see. Anyway, my own life is family tattle, right?"

"Indeed. I mean no, Lady. A large portion of them are attentive, and those of us who've been with you for some time ensure that whatever is said will be said consciously. Of that, you can be guaranteed. A few of us – we've effectively conversed with Roberto."

Amelia caused a stir.

"We don't endure anybody speaking discourteously about you. You're our lord, and you're additionally my kinswoman. However, what might be said about Captain Fisher? He cherishes you, you know." She turned away. "He hasn't taken a gander at any other individual in quite a while."

"He adores me? Did he disclose to you this? How long have you known this, Jaime?" she requested discreetly. "How long?"

Jaime looked down in disgrace. "Just about two years now."

"Two years!" Amelia took a long breath. "As you just reminded me, you are my kinswoman and promised to serve and watch my House. You made vows of loyalty to care for my inclinations as though they were your own. Whatever had you to stay quiet about such from me?"

"He has served you well, and he is the commander of your gatekeeper and my predominant official. He requested me to quiet." Jaime looked into, seeing the anger and double-crossing in her Mistress' eyes. She gradually dropped to her knees. "Wh-how will you deal with him?"

Amelia took a gander at her strangely. "No words for yourself?"

Jaime looked broke, destroys running her cheeks. "No, Lady. I have no reason. It's your entitlement to rebuff and excuse me shamefully."

"I'm angry. However, I realize enough not to follow up on that rage. Get out."

Jaime gazed upward dreadfully. "It is safe to say that you will charge him?"

So that is what I resembled, Amelia thought. However, I see no uncertainty in her eyes. She couldn't care less about herself, just him. Is it true that she is infatuated with him, as well? The subsequent adage came unbidden to her contemplations: Love can't be constrained or shackled and persevere. It emerges unlooked for, and in disobedience of all explanation or result, goes where it will. Amelia dismissed. "No, I'm not going to charge him. Presently get out, Jaime, before I accomplish something, we'll both lament!"

Jaime mixed to her feet and rushed out, leaving the entryway unlatched.

Amelia breathed out, at that point, went over and sat on the edge of her bed. Her normal psyche fought with her heart. She knew whether Brandon left her administration, she'd likely lose Jaime also. Other than the anguish of losing two individuals, she thought about companions; there was additionally the political danger. Battle with the mythical foresty people appeared to be a genuine chance. Amelia shut her eyes. On the off chance that it worked out that Brandon didn't adore her, he truly would need to leave. She would suggest them both so that some other House would have their abilities.

Ten years.

When she conceded she cherished him, she realized she needed to be held in Brandon's solid arms by and by. She needed to feel him inside her, yet more than that, to rest in a similar bed close to him and wake up adjacent to him. She needed his kids.

Pregnant.

Tia likewise revealed to her she planned to have a kid, and Brandon was the dad. Tia had then inquired as to whether she needed the spell to affirm it. Amelia realized it wasn't required. She'd been around her mom enough not to address how or why clerics knew things.

No. If she could not have Brandon, she would lament, yet she'd let him abandon malignance. What her little girl would do, Amelia challenged not to abide upon.

On edge, she stood up and started to pace.

If he admitted his adoration and how stupid he'd been, it would soothe her harmed pride. On the off chance that he responded to her inquiries sufficiently, she would propose to him today. Custom held that whoever was top of the family at that point served in the room. Like her folks, a few relationships were genuine associations, even though her mom had surrendered her House name and her position as princess upon her marriage. Amelia realized she would be glad to have Brandon as her accomplice or run with him as an associate. Be that as it may, she would not wed into his House, with him as top of the family. Amelia was resolved to keep her entitlement to manage the duchy.

She shook her head—no more deferrals. The pressure among her and Brandon had been working for quite a while. Whatever the completion, the dam had blasted, and the deluges had effectively left harmed afterward. Best to wrap it up, presently, before more passionate losses were asserted.

Amelia stomped out of her room and down to his office.

Two raps outside, a respite, at that point, she flung open the entryway.

He was situated in his seat, gazing out the window. He turned when she entered. A day's development of facial hair growth all over, and it seemed as though he had dozed close to nothing if by any means. A piece of her was glad to see he fared more regrettable; however, another piece of her needed to hold and solace him. Amelia shut the entryway. "Great. You're here."

Brandon gestured.

She put her hands on her hips. "For what reason did you do it, Brandon?"

"I have no reason, Lady Amelia," he addressed unobtrusively. "I will keep your judgment, whatever you choose."

"I don't need reasons or servility, damn it! Answer my inquiry! Why?"

"I was unable to stand the possibility of you being with another man."

Her heart jumped. All the more unobtrusively, she said, "For what reason didn't you simply ask me?"

"Would you have said yes?"

"Possibly! I don't know since I wasn't inquired! For what reason wouldn't you be able to stand me being with another man, Brandon? Advise me!"

"Since I love you, Amelia. I see you, and I would prefer not to be with any other person. I realized we were unable to be together, yet when I saw you in that blue dress, publicizing your craving, your status for sex and a kid, I needed to have you."

Euphoria filled her. "You love me? I–what? Stand by a moment." Amelia came around the work area and inclined close. "For what reason wouldn't we be able to be together?"

Brandon gazed toward her. "Since I guaranteed your dad I could never look for your hand. I was picked to secure you. Your dad was correct, as well. Also, I wouldn't be content except if we were hitched."

Amelia felt the warmth race to her face. She brushed his unpleasant cheek. "Wouldn't you say I'm mature enough to settle on my own choices? I went through the Rite of Adulthood, which demonstrated I am equipped for settling on my own life and passing decisions. My dad may have chosen you. However, you made your vow of administration to me, Brandon Fisher. It wasn't appropriate for him to ask that, and it wasn't ideal for you to keep that guarantee from me." She kissed his temple. "We've both gone through a great deal of torment in light of this mystery between us." She kissed each cheek, her hot breath like a brand across his face. "I love you, as well, Brandon. I need you to be my better half. If you wish, I can co-join our Houses and take the name of Starshine-Fisher. Our children will bear your House name, and our little girls will bear mine." Her mouth brushed his lips once, twice, at that point kissing him wildly, slid onto his lap.

Brandon's arms folded over her, reacting in kind.

Following a few minutes, they fell to pieces, breathing intensely.

"Is that a yes?" she husked.

He investigated her eyes mindfully, gesturing. "A kiss. So now we are authoritatively sweethearts, yes? To impart capacity to you is enticing; however, no. After your folks are gone, you need to lead the duchy, don't you?" When he saw the faltering in her eyes, he immediately consoled her. "Amelia, I've served you for quite a while, and I am substance to keep our outside relationship, all things considered, with you in control. You are a brilliant lady, conceived and prepared to run the show. You will be Duchess, and I will serve you as your Lord Consort." Brandon slipped his arm under her legs, handily rose with her in his arms, at that point sat her onto the edge of the work area. He stroked her cheek tenderly. "You thus acknowledge what that will mean? That between us, I will be expert, and you will serve me in our bed?"

Flushing, she gestured. "Indeed, Brandon. We are concurred on the terms of marriage, at that point? I will lead the House and the Duchy, and like this, I promise my body to your pleasure in our bed." As he remained before her, her hands ran here and there his chest.

Fulfillment filled his face. "To have you at whatever point I need? I will be exceptionally content with that game plan."

His hands lifted her dress over her hips, and he pulled down her underwear. Amelia lifted to make it simpler, gnawing her lower lip in expectation. As of now, she felt herself releasing and developing wet.

"I have two solicitations before we have an arrangement. Take out my rooster, Amelia. Furthermore, no, that wasn't one of the solicitations."

Astounded, she inclined forward and fixed his belt and fastens, at that point pushed his jeans down.

He stroked her hair. "To start with, I need your dad's delivery from my guarantee."

She inclined toward his stroke, murmuring. "Obviously. You made a vow to him, isn't that right? Also, you wish to act respectably by the two of us. After I disclose my emotions to him, I question he will hold us up, particularly when I make my own emotions understood. The other?"

Amelia inclined forward to his developing erection, giving it a speedy lick before bringing him into her mouth. Hearing his wheeze of delight expanded her hunger. Her tongue lathed his pulsating organ, making it as wet as could be expected. At that point, she sat up, and he pushed ahead between her legs. Reclining, she guided him to the passage of her sex.

"The following condition. I need your approval to embrace Dalyanni. I love her, and she needs a dad. I need you as my significant other. However, I additionally need her for my little girl." He pushed against her delicate, wet tissue yet didn't enter.

Dalyanni would at long last have the dad she hungered for. Amelia looked at him, overpowered with adoration and unexpected, great desire. "On the off chance that she says indeed, you have my approval." She snared her legs around him. Coming down, she spread her labia around his crown at her passage and, utilizing her legs, pulled him closer. "It is safe to say that we are concurred and done? Since, in such a case that you don't take me at present, I figure I may shout."

Smiling, his face loaded with want, Brandon bumped once, and afterward a second, an ideal opportunity for profundity.

She gasped and afterward moaned, feeling the totality of his essence pushing into her. She touched his unpleasant face, wondering with shock at how great he felt. "Brandon, you might have had me numerous years prior, yet you decided to disregard my clues. Gracious, my, you feel better. Try not to take me wrong. However,

I need to know. Mmmm. What made you alter your perspective?"

His face gentled, his profound testing moderate and simple. "It was August, right around two years prior. We were visiting your folks for your sister's birthday. It was late evening, chilling following a blistering day. You were in the nursery with your mom and Dalyanni. You wore your House colors that day."

Amelia gestured, reviewing the occasion.

"Dalyanni discovered some bug and took it to you. You hungover to address her. Your grin, loaded with adoration, the sun sparkling off your face and brilliant light hair gleaming in the sun's light. You blew my mind. I thought you the most perfectly brilliant lady on the planet. That was the point at which I could presently don't deny my affections for you."

"Say–say my name, Brandon. Advise me–unh–reveal to me you love me."

Pounding his pelvis against hers, he inclined down, breathing the words onto her face. "I love you, Amelia Starshine. I love you. I don't mind who you were with yesterday–"

"I didn't," she dissented.

He stopped, pausing.

She up saw him, attempting to make him comprehend. "I proved unable. Not after that. I needed to figure things out first."

Brandon gestured as he continued moving inside her smooth warmth. "You're correct, Amelia. The mysterious hurt us both, and I'm upset for the agony I caused you. I have a couple of different insider facts I need to share–"

An abrupt look of alert moved quickly over her face. "You're not hitched, right?"

"What?" Then he snickered. "No, I'm not hitched; however, I plan to cure that as quickly as time permits,

Amelia. The insider facts aren't time-touchy, yet you should know them in any case. Genuineness between a future couple is something to be thankful for. You need youngsters?"

The paradox of the inquiry made Amelia smile. She lifted and kissed him. "Gracious, yes." For accentuation, she put her feet at the little of his back, crushing him tighter and shaking her hips against his pushing, delighting in his development inside her stimulated, smooth focus.

He smiled back. "That is the thing that I needed to hear, Amelia. I will make a valiant effort to offer them to you. For the following a little while, a few times each day, I will take you. Some of them will be brisk, and some will keep you occupied for quite a long time." At that, he moved all the more overwhelmingly.

Amelia moaned and tore separated his shirt, sending catches flying. She ran her hands over his naked chest, at that point, delved her fingernails into his arms. Brandon expanded his speed, his hips slapping boisterous and wet as he pistoned into her. Delight flooded, conveying Amelia nearer to joy. Out of nowhere, he snorted and pushed profound, granulating against her.

"Try not to stop," she whimpered. "Please!" Her hands held further as she kicked and shook against him.

Abruptly understanding, Brandon continued pushing, his section smooth from the semen effectively somewhere inside her.

In under a moment, she angled her back and froze, her hands and legs holding him like a tight clamp. "Goodness, God!" she heaved, at that point, pulled him down for a kiss, granulating her pulsating sex around him. As the waves lessened and the air requirement developed, she at long last let him go, heaving. "Gracious, that was acceptable! Mmm, goodness – gracious, yes."

"This is the place where you should be, Amelia. Actually, like this."

She flushed with shame and delight. At the point when she felt him start to move once more, she gazed upward in shock. "OK, I'm dazzled. I can go once again, yet no more. You must give me a possibility, Husband, to become acclimated to such an excess of coupling."

He smiled. "All good. 'Spouse.' I like hearing you say that, Wife."

"This capacity of yours. Is this one of your insider facts?" Her hand followed his cheek and jawline, at that point his ear.

Brandon grasped her hand and kissed it. "Indeed."

Amelia lay back on the work area, watching his face and getting a charge out of the impression of him moving inside her body, yet additionally contemplating how regularly she would submit him. He said they a few times each day to give her the kid she needed. She had needed an ordinary darling in the most exceedingly terrible manner for a long time. Regardless of the new occasions, she cherished him. All the disappointment and strain that had been between them was disappearing. All things considered, if he had mysteries, she had her own.

It was then she had an egotistical idea. She needed kids, and he needed to oblige her. Amelia came to up and licked his areolas, in a steady progression, to and fro, flicking them with her tongue, at that point snacking with her teeth. "Offer it to me, Brandon. Do me once more. Fill me with your seed. I need everything."

Brandon moaned and compensated her by grasping her backside, crashing hard into her, rotating from one side to another, at that point overwhelmingly siphoning into her open, sopping sex.

Amelia held tight, smiling as she gasped in joy, in adoration, and inebriated by his maleness. The delight of having a darling and being wanted. His being inside her, filling her, separating her. The delightful feel of his shaft running the profundity of her wet community. The musky smell and the soft commotions of coupling. The pleasantness of pressure building and the inescapable, magnificent delivery. She was clumsy, however, anxious to compensate for some recent setbacks. Also, a short time later, to be held in his arms? Allow Brandon to put forth a valiant effort by her. What could it hurt, she pondered, to stand by a month or two preceding saying anything?

CPSIA information can be obtained
at www.ICGtesting.com
Printed in the USA
BVHW062048050421
604208BV00003B/581